He Who Expecteth
Never Receiveth

HE WHO EXPECTETH NEVER RECEIVETH

Recollections of a boy growing up in the 1940s/50s

by

Freddie Harris

Central Publishing Services
United Kingdom

Paperback 1 904908 25 X

Produced
by

Central Publishing Services
Royd Street Offices
Milnsbridge
Huddersfield
West Yorkshire
HD3 4QY

www.centralpublishing.co.uk

Growing up in the 1940s/50s was not all doom, gloom and hardship, although much of it was for the less well off. Fun was to be had if one created it, as recreation in those days was mostly self-generated. This book tries to bring to the reader some of the lighter side of life as it was, through the experiences of one whose childhood spanned that period. The back entry playgrounds, the gangs, the bonfires and school activities, along with other childhood activities, are all remembered with amusement, and a little sadness.

***

Author's note:

This story is part fiction but has basis in fact. It is a tongue in cheek tale recalling my formative years and, in the main, the events described actually happened. I have exercised my right to use artistic licence to enhance the storyline, but I leave it to the reader to decide what is fact, and what is fiction. The suburb of Manchester referred to as Upshaw exists only in my imagination, as do some of the other locations mentioned. I have also changed the names of persons involved to protect anonymity. Whilst conversations cannot be recalled verbatim over a period of more than half a century, they would have been very much as I have recorded them, if, in fact, they ever took place at all.

***

ACKNOWLEDGEMENT

My thanks go to Joyce Hill for her help and suggestions whilst I was putting this book together. To Paul Riding for his assistance with the computer and Esme Monks for making sure I did not lose all I had written! But most of all I could not have completed this book without the help of my wife who dotted every 'i', crossed every 't' and made sure ·it all made sense. Your encouragement and patience made my pleasurable task so much easier. Thank you all.

***

He Who Expecteth

1

The troops were coming at me thick and fast. I felt I was drowning, engulfed in a sea of khaki and unable to do anything about it. Panic was beginning to set in and I felt my limbs go stiff. The scene was one of wild confusion, pandemonium almost, with bodies shooting off in all directions. This was not the Somme or any other battle theatre of Europe but London Road Railway Station in Manchester and we were here to meet dad returning home from World War Two.

It was 1946. I was two and a half years old and was being held in the arms of a woman whom I found out later was my mother, being pushed towards iron railing, where the soldiers were milling around seeking out their loved ones. They had disembarked from a huge, black, smoking monster that scared the hell out of me, and a man with a face covered in coal dust winked in my direction from the cab of the beast and I thought he was 'old nick'. I don't know if he was winking at my mother or me but he still gives me nightmares if I think about him too much.

I had never seen my dad, I being born in January 1944, whilst he had gone to fight the Germans in 1940. Quite how I came to be born is still a mystery to me, but he must have nipped home at some stage because I look so much like him there is no mistaking that I am his son. Mother held me forward with outstretched arms and said, "Give daddy a kiss." My reaction was to bawl the station down.

There was a bus queue with a multitude of people lining up for what I was told was the last bus out of town. It was like the Tribe of Israel waiting their turn to cross the Red Sea, or it could have been the Catholics on their way to midnight mass because it was dark. If it was the Israelites then Moses wasn't doing a very good job, because everyone was jockeying for the most advantageous position. They all wanted to cross the Red Sea before it was too late. Despite the turmoil, the soldier with his wife and child were shepherded to the front, by an act of sheer compassion I am sure, and apparently made it home that night.

***

There is an aphorism that says, '*It's hard to remember that your initial intention was to drain the swamp when you are up to your backside in alligators.*' I do not know who first articulated this adage and it's of trifling relevance anyway but the fact remains that it seems to fit my childhood. Not that we lived in the jungle or the everglades you understand. The back streets of Upshaw where I was born and brought up is a suburb of Manchester and a far cry from the imaginary grandeur of such places. Imagination I had in plenty and used it to escape what was my 'lot'. I was not particularly enamoured with what providence had laid out for me. Being one of ten kids (five boys, five girls), was not what I would have chosen had I been given a free hand. My minds eye had me as the son of nobility able to do just as I pleased, or a film star living it up on the Riviera, a far cry from the back entries of Upshaw. I was determined to get away, or 'drain the swamp', but the alligators were the reality and had a firm grip. In 'Lady Windermere's Fan', Oscar Wilde wrote, *'We are all in the gutter, but some of us are looking at the stars.'* He was quite obviously thinking of me when he wrote this. If this sounds ungrateful then I was ungrateful.

Gratitude. That feeling of being thankful for a favour or a gift. Why should I feel gratitude to a set of circumstances! That's why I'm here, because of a set of circumstances, not as a result of a favour or a gift. I wasn't planned; in fact I do not think that I was even wanted, more like an intrusion into someone else's private world. I do not ever recall being told I was loved by anyone throughout my entire childhood. I was a snotty nosed little kid who got in the way of everything or I would have done had my parents allowed me to get in the way at all.

In truth, I was too quiet, too reticent and stifled to be an obstacle to anyone. That was probably my trouble. Had I been more flamboyant, a little more verbal and outward going like my next elder brother John, then perhaps my boyhood years would not have been so laboured. "Freddie go for this; Freddie go for that; Freddie do the dishes; Freddie look after your younger sisters; Freddie do your early morning milk round; Freddie do your after school paper round." Give me a brush and I'll stick it up my backside and clean the yard whilst I am at it, was the thought that I nurtured. The life of a serf was not one full of gratitude.

It appeared to me that I was the only one in the family to be at mother's beck and call, although in reality this, of course, was not the case. My elder sisters also had their chores and many tasks to perform in and around the household, but when you are young you see yourself as the only victim of tyrannical potency.

Mother's whole life seemed to be centred on the back street bookie's shop whilst dad, when not at work or asleep, was either in the Legion or the Working Men's Club. He worked bloody hard in the steel works for most of the week, so felt his leisure times could be spent how he liked. Maybe he was right. Twelve hour shifts, often for seven days a week was a lot to ask of anyone.

I can still hear my mother hollering down our back alley or 'entry' as we used to call it, butting into my imaginary world of Batman and Robin, or Dan Dare that superstar from the future. "Freddie, go down to George French's and see if I have any returns." George French was our local back street bookmaker, illegal of course in those days, but his kind could be found in plenty if you knew where to look. 'Returns' were any monies mother had won that day on the horses. Gamblers' Anonymous was tailor made for my mother, not that she would for one moment have contemplated such an idea, but games of chance really were at the forefront of her mind to the detriment of most else. Bingo; football pools; spot the ball; dog racing; anything would do so long as you had a chance of making a fortune, which, of course, very few people ever did. How I looked forward to the days when no racing took place. It is no wonder I grew up with an abhorrence to gambling and am teetotal.

Mother used to write her bets on any old piece of paper that was lying around, a piece of Shredded Wheat box or sugar wrapping, or even crayoned on that old shiny toilet paper, unused of course. She did not always pay cash up front for her bets but had them on credit from time to time and would pay at the end of the week if enough funds were available. Any winnings would be deducted from what she owed, but winnings were very few and far between. Many a week ended in tears because she could not meet the bookie's demands. Dad rarely knew of any of these transactions.

In my role as bookie's runner I would gallop down Folton Road in the direction of the CWS soap works on my imaginary horse, with my cardboard mask and a cape, made from an old curtain one of the neighbours had 'cobbed' in the bin, flying out behind me. Quite what Batman or Dan Dare was doing on a horse seemed to be unimportant at the time. I would shout obscenities at the Catholic kids who frolicked in the playground of the English Martyrs' school near the bookie's shop, then run like the wind in case any of them got over the railings to 'put me right'. Well everybody did it. It was the 'done thing'. My father was a Catholic, 'though non-practising, but I did not let that stop me. God I was fearless!

The bookie's shop was a little room over an indoor flea market and the stairway leading up to it gave me the creeps.

It was dark and dirty and if the bogey man lived anywhere then it was along the corridor that shot off to the left at the top of the stairs. On this passageway hung a well worn poster advertising 'Ogden's Midnight Flake' which showed a queue of people at a railway station ticket office window. It put me in mind of those people in Manchester who were waiting to cross the Red Sea. To draw the attention of the bookie, one had to knock on an unmarked door and a little panel would open inward, just like the pictures I had seen of the 'speak easy' houses in prohibition America. A face would appear and the mouth would say, "O.K., it is only Freddie." That part I liked. I pretended to be a gangster and put on my meanest look as I handed over the betting slip. How I must have impressed the clerk.

My mother was not what one might call energetic. In fact, she rarely rose before mid-day despite having been awake for hours. You could, in mitigation, say that having presented the world with ten children had taken its toll and drained her of energy, but this was off-set by the fact that she was never too tired to go out to the Legion for an evening of drinking and bingo playing. Anyway, Mrs Jackson down the road had produced fifteen worthies and was up to see them off to school every day, and Mrs O'Sullivan next door to her had twelve and was still able to attend holy mass at the crack of dawn every morning, then carry out a full day's work. No, the truth was my mother was somewhat less than energetic.

Saturday morning was the time the hire purchase transactions took place. Mother would lie in bed, the brown handbag with camels imprinted on it by her side. Dad had brought this home with him from Egypt after the war, and she used it as a holder for the higher purchase paying in books. We had many items on higher purchase as did most working class people in those days, and two bob a week was the going rate. She would select the lucky ones to be paid that week (some usually had to be left unpaid because insufficient funds were available) by putting a two shilling piece on top of each book. There always seemed to be a pram in our back garden so Ridgeway's Pram shop was always on the list of creditors, along with Ridings Furniture Store. After I had made her a cup of tea and taken it up to her, it was my job then to visit the shops being paid, and as this task normally took about an hour, playing out, flying to the moon with Flash Gordon or climbing Mount Everest with Sherpa Tenzing Norgay had to wait. From then on I was free to do as I pleased until the horse racing started in the afternoon, when I would stand by for a call to gallop off to George French, Turf Accountant's Office.

***

I was the seventh child. They say the seventh child is always different and I do not think I contradicted this theory. I always felt at variance with the rest of the family. In fact, when I was ten or eleven, I was convinced I had been adopted and had not lived up to the expectations of my adopted parents and that's why I was being given the rough end of the stick. How daft can you be to think that a working class family on low income and six kids already would adopt another one. Daft or not, logic played only a bit part in my early years. I was not the brightest button on the coat.

I was left out of so much that was going on in the family I think I actually became paranoid. I remember being told to look after the house whilst everyone else went off to church to see our Lana get married to Frank. "You can come to the 'do' in the parlour afterwards," I was told. I never got to the 'do' in the parlour afterwards because everyone was getting a bit worse for wear with the drink and my grannie said I should not be exposed to such goings on.

Grannie lived about a mile away but spent most of her time at our place. One day when my mum was out, she put a bowl on my head and cut my hair because she said I looked like a scruff. So I had the 'Beatle Cut' long before they did and have a photograph to prove it. When our Neil and Nora had a double wedding I was again left at home because there were so many people going to the church, it being a three family affair, that I would only get in the way.

I played in the entry until it was all over and then went to bed just like a normal day. Our Rodney, who was four years younger, went because he was the baby of the family at that time, and everybody likes to see the baby even if he is three years old.

When my grannie died, they took her to be interred at Allerton cemetery in Liverpool but I was left behind because it was too far for me to travel. Our Rodney went because he was too young to be left on his own, whereas I was quite capable of playing out until they returned.

One day my Auntie Dolly took a bunch of children to Belle Vue, the zoo and fairground in Manchester, but once again I was left for reasons I can no longer remember, but I know it hurt because our John and Daisy both went. On another occasion, Uncle Bill, who was not a real uncle but a friend of my dad, came up for the day from Liverpool where he lived. I cannot remember what was being celebrated but after a goodly dinner time session in the Legion, the party continued in our front parlour with many of dad's friends invited to join in. A sing-song got under way and everyone was enjoying a carefree afternoon, all except me who had been sent out to play in the entry. Some time in the afternoon, I was called to go to the back door of the Legion where the steward had a box of Guinness for me to bring home. On delivering the box, which weighed a ton, I was given a sixpenny piece from Uncle Bill who was a kind man, and was sent on my way. There were many more occasions, too numerous to record, and the fact remains I felt like a pariah at home for most of my childhood.

***

2

Life was not easy in the forties and fifties for a working class family. The Second World War had kicked the hell out of everybody and most of my pals knew some sort of hardship. I will not call them friends because I did not make friends easily and still do not. I am not sure why. Perhaps it has something to do with being disappointed or let down, or not being able to give as much as one would like. Maybe it's the fact that if you do not let anyone in, you will not be hurt. One friend I did have in those days was a Polish refugee who had been given a decidedly rough time by Herr Hitler. After a short period in a 'Misplaced Persons Camp', Archie Konecheni, (I do not know the correct spelling of his name but, never mind, neither did he), came to our house at irregular intervals for food and shelter. He had come to know our family through dad's connection with the British Legion. It was always a delight for me to see his massive frame appear in our entry. At least it had been massive at one time but, now in his mid twenties, the hardship was beginning to show.

How I loved that man. When funds allowed he would

put me on his broad shoulders and off we would gallop to the local fleapit to see the latest offering Hollywood had so graciously provided for our entertainment. He was always so full of fun with us young ones despite his misfortune.

It was through this huge, handsome, blonde haired Pole that I first heard the word 'delicatessen'. He tried numerous times to get me to pronounce the word correctly but eventually gave up saying, "I vos a lozt korz." Funny how unimportant things stick with you. Work was not easy to find, especially for a misplaced person and the Government was not as free with our money in those days as it is today. What did it matter if

Archie and thousands like him suffered. So what if he did go hungry. He was just another victim of man's stupidity. The world was free, was it not? Free – ha! I loved that man so much, I would have given him my last crust of bread and I know he would have done the same for me. He did

occasionally find work washing dishes in back street cafes but this never lasted for long.

When he came to our house, he would often cut himself a slice of bread and thicken it with 'Maggie Ann' (margarine) and my eyes would bulge in envy. How I wished I could have been allowed to do the same thing. This was before the introduction of sliced bread and his slices were enormous. We would refer to them as 'dockers' wedges', a term that had Archie in fits of laughter because I doubt he ever knew what 'dockers' wedges' were. How I loved to see him laugh. God knows, if anyone deserved to laugh it was my big Polish hero. Well, he was a hero to me and that is all that mattered. I remember him offering marriage to my eldest sister Lana but she turned him down because, amongst other reasons, she was walking out with a local man called Frank whom she would eventually marry. One wonders how long marriage to Archie would have lasted.

Like so many others, Archie did not have a place in the world he had given so much to create. He had little English and his work skills had been those of a farm labourer until fate took over and shoved a rifle in his jumbo sized fists. I can still see the old photograph of Archie in Polish Army uniform standing next to a mud-splattered tank. I remember him telling me how he feared and hated the Russians and the Germans for the atrocities they had committed on his kinsfolk and his homeland. Archie died cold, hungry and alone in a shop doorway in Manchester, too dejected and weary to carry on, and that makes me sad. He was just twenty-eight years old.

***

They tell me I was a good child and never asked or longed for anything. Lana told me I was a joy to take out and never gave any bother whatsoever, no matter where I was taken. If I was shown toys or nice clothing, like sailor suits that were all the go for young boys in those days , I would say things like, "They're too expensive for us," and walk on without fuss or commotion. I never kicked up or cried, asked to be carried or misbehaved in any way, which made me a little goody two shoes.

Lana was courting Frank and I would be about three years old at the time. They decided they would have a day out at New Brighton on the Wirral, a favourite seaside spot in those days, but sadly no longer, and they would take me with them seeing as I was so good and quiet. The route was by train to Liverpool, a tram ride to the Pier Head and the ferry across the Mersey (now didn't someone write a song about that?) to the seaside resort. The tram car ride was a great thrill and made a whirring noise like no other sound on earth. It trundled down the centre of the road, rocking this way and that, with people scampering to get out of its path. The ding, ding of the conductor's bell added to the hustle and bustle of the jaunt, with people dashing to their place of work, or their appointment with the ferry boat.

A notice on the tram read, 'No Spitting Allowed', but I do not remember this as being one of my habits. "Pier Head," the conductor shouted, which was our cue to get off and join the line of day trippers waiting on the floating dock. On the boat across Frank sat me on the rail overlooking the sea and I remember stiffening in stark terror even though he had tight hold of me and there was no chance of me falling in. When I found my senses, I bawled my head off until the threat of a watery grave was removed. Lana said afterwards it was the first time I had cried since meeting dad coming home from war, but the day was yet young.

The pleasure beach had one of those big dipper things, built to put the fear of Christ into three year old boys, so I did not let him down. If God had meant you to be that high he would have given you the ability to fly, but that did not stop our Lana and Frank. Into the carriage we went creeping slowly to the top. Somebody then took my breath away, pushed my stomach into my mouth and hurled me downwards towards the ground which I left only a few moments before. This I did not consider as entertainment and decided to do another bawling act. Two in one day, this was unheard of.

Later that afternoon, after being taken on more sedate swings and roundabouts, I spotted a tin drum on a side stall and decided I had to have it. It cost two bob (10p) which was exactly what Lana and Frank had left between them and the workhouse. It was getting near home time and the return boat was waiting to ferry us back to Liverpool but I wanted my drum. I cried my eyes out until Frank had heard enough and decided he would spend their combined remaining wealth on the tin drum. They had the return tickets home so what the hell.

As the train approached Upshaw Station, it became apparent it was not going to stop. They had inadvertently got on the non stopper from Liverpool to Manchester and the latter was where they finished up. They had no money now to get back to Upshaw because my blasted drum had used up the remaining funds. A ten mile walk with a three year old child and a new drum was not a pleasurable prospect. A sympathetic station master at Manchester took pity on them and gave them a free ride back to Upshaw on the next 'stopper'. I was not taken on 'days out' for quite a while after that, and I have never been on the big dipper since. I did, however, become quite a proficient drummer.

***

Before the Nunn family moved into the house next door, it was inhabited by an ancient couple by the name of Heyams. Mrs Heyams produced vast quantities of home made jam. This was hard and crystal like and had to be chewed, if one was unfortunate enough to be given a jar or two, which we were on numerous occasions. This sounds unappreciative but I wish she had not bothered because my mum insisted that we had it on our bread and she did not care if it did make us balk. We would damn well have it and like it. But the main reason I remember the Heyams is because of something that occurred after they died, a phenomenon which was witnessed by my brother John and myself.

Let me explain. The Heyams slept in the bedroom that was back to back with the one our John and I shared, and every morning one of them wheeled their bed across the lino covered floor to the window, presumably to air it out. It was an old, iron bedstead which made a very loud, squeaky noise that drove us mad so early in the morning, usually before we had arisen. They rose at the crack of dawn each day, having done so since they were young due to their working in the mills in Bolton. They told me this many times.

They died within weeks of each other and, having no family or near relatives, the house remained empty for a considerable length of time. However, their death did not stop the bed from being rolled across the room every morning even though no one was in the house and it was locked up. This squeaking continued for several weeks and every time I mentioned it to my mum I was told not to be so stupid. They were dead and that was that . Even our John could get no one to believe us and I had given up trying until one morning mum heard it for herself and informed Inspector Harrington, the local police chief, who was a mate of my dad. The Inspector had the house opened and checked over by a couple of his men but nothing untoward was found. Everything was in order, including the bed, which was not by the window but in the centre of the room where it should have been. This bed squealing noise was heard on several later occasions by both John and me but we did not bother mentioning it again and got quite used to it. It did eventually stop before the Nunns took residence and I offer no explanation as to why or how it ever happened.

***

3

Now 'Gormless Gregory', there was a boy for you. Gormless Gregory lived in the last house in the square at the end of our back entry. We called him 'gormless' because that is what he was. A genuine jackass, who could not tie his own shoelaces, write his own name and had a face that would frighten Quasimodo. The local neighbourhood dogs used to run home howling when Gregory put in an appearance. My Grannie's clock stopped one day after ticking for over a century without fault, and she maintained to her dying day that it was because Gregory had pulled tongues at it. I believed that story for years. Grannie did not like Gregory, saying, "He wasn't fit to live with pigs." I, of course, stood up for him and said he was!

The young girls of the area were terrified of him. He was only small in stature and had the hint of a hunchback, just like that geezer from Notre Dame, but what power he possessed. I kept 'well in' with him because he was good at nicking things and I was not. He always managed to produce enough pennies to get into the kids' matinee on a

Saturday afternoon and enough to purchase an ice lollypop as well, which was another good reason for being his pal. He never said where that money came from and I never asked, but I do know that he was a dirty little beggar who would show his willy to anyone for three pence. So maybe his willy took me to all those matinees - who cares!

His father was also small and walked with a very pronounced limp. Somebody said when he was young he tried to give an injection to a horse, but the horse moved and he injected himself and that is why he limped. We all believed this and gave Gregory's dad a wide berth in case he wanted to get his revenge on the horse population and used us as surrogate mustangs. Quite why a boiler man in the steel works would be giving an injection to horse never occurred to us.

Gormless would go into the small corner shop at the end of our entry whilst the rest of the gang waited on the cobbles outside. He would re-appear after a few minutes and produce from under his scruffy jumper a packet of chocolate biscuits or some other delectation unobtainable to us by honest means. We would devour these with great gusto whilst riding the swings in the local park. He was never mean with his stolen goods I will say that for him. He smoked like a chimney, spat whenever and wherever he felt like it and never washed. This made Gregory somewhat of a hero figure and he was known throughout the district. What eminence!

He was an only child. I think his parents probably looked at him when he was born and said "Why us?", and decided that to chance providence any further would be foolhardy. His mother was a lovely woman who always wore a turban and for years we all thought this meant she belonged to a secret society of some kind. She never once shouted for Gregory to go to George French's to see if there were any returns, which made her rather special in my eyes. In fact, she was such a quiet woman the only time you saw her was when she slipped out of the house to the corner shop for a quarter of tea or something, the same corner shop Gormless nicked our biscuits from.

Gregory taught himself to play the guitar he said he had stolen from a shop on King Street in Manchester, but you never quite knew when he was telling the truth or was just trying to enhance his reputation as a reprobate. When he grew up he played the guitar professionally and backed such people as the Everley Brothers, Roy Orbison, Guy Mitchell and many other big name stars. Just goes to show that if you are an ugly, hunched back thief with dirty habits and a father who limps you can still make it in life.

***

Dick Head Dennis was cast in the same mould as Gregory, though not as obnoxious. He was quite selective where he spat. We called him Dick Head because his face resembled the male sex organ. Well we thought it did anyway. He always walked as if he was drunk because he thought this made him look hard and did it to impress us lesser mortals. It did not work because we all thought that he was a prat. Dennis's saving grace was that he was a good football player. This made him a little more acceptable especially to the sports master at school who knew nothing except how to kick a football. Mr. Chapples was his name and it was rumoured that he could not read or write and did not know where France was. I cannot remember why France was important but that was the word in the playground.

Dick Head did not live in our neck of the woods and was not really in our gang, but would suddenly appear in the back entry like an apparition. It was quite a while before I found out where he did live and I was impressed because it was relatively posh. They had leaded windows and carpets on the floors, which really put him out of my league, but for some reason he liked our end of town.

I remember Dick Head mainly because he introduced me to coffee. I called around for him one afternoon to go for a game of football on the meadows because he owned a proper football. He was not quite ready so invited me in. "Help yourself to a coffee," he said. "Just put a spoonful of that brown stuff in a mug and pour hot water on it," he told me. The brown stuff Dick Head had pointed to was on the kitchen worktop, and turned out to be a jar of Nescafe. We didn't have worktops in our kitchen. We had a pull down opening to a food cabinet used for almost everything from cutting bread to rolling out pastry for home made pies our Daisy seemed to specialise in. I had seen these coffee jars in the shops, of course, but had never actually held one. We occasionally had a bottle of 'Camp' at home which was a mixture of chicory essence and coffee and was bitter and offensive to my taste buds, but pure coffee would be a first for me.

I reached out for the jar and grabbed it by the lid, not realising the lid was unscrewed. The jar and its contents fell from my grasp. By a nifty piece of footwork I managed to stop the jar smashing on the kitchen floor, but could do nothing to save the coffee spilling all over the place. "Everything O.K.," Dick Head shouted on hearing the commotion. I lied and assured him everything was splendid, as I hunted for a brush to sweep up the mess that now covered the rather muddy kitchen floor. It had been raining that morning and my mucky shoes had done nothing to improve the cleanliness of the quarry tiles that lay underfoot.

Finding a hand brush and shovel in a cupboard under the sink, I set to rectifying the disorder caused by my clumsiness. The stuff seemed to have gone everywhere and I was very glad that Dick Head's mother was out shopping. Eventually I gathered up the offending coffee grains along with traces of mud and lord knows what else from the kitchen floor, but what could I do with this debris now. I looked at the jar and saw it was almost empty. Crikey, Mrs Dick Head would go spare. The colour of the stuff on the shovel did not look quite the same as the coffee remaining in the jar, but I decided there was only one thing I could do. Having managed to pick out a few hairs and other foreign bodies, that had intermingled with the coffee grains, I emptied the contents of the shovel back into the coffee jar and shock it up.

Good as new I thought, but there was a problem. Dennis had offered me a drink and I had accepted, and besides, I had never tasted real coffee. The only thing to do was to brave it out and get stuck in. I piled a spoonful of the mixture into a mug and added hot water. Delicious. Dick Head then appeared and grabbed hold of my arm stating it was time for our game before it got dark. I told him to be careful as he had almost made me spill my coffee. "Don't do that for heaven's sake or mum will go mad. She hates anyone messing in her kitchen, especially since she has had the new tiles put down," he said. We left then before his mum returned, with me picking bits out of my mouth and wondering what they would make of their 'improved' jar of Nescafe. I never did find out.

***

Mrs. Long was very short, about 4ft 3in, and had to stand on an orange box to see over the counter in the sweet shop she ran. She wore a white pinafore and a little white hat that looked like a doily. We thought she was very mean as well as very short because she would not allow us any more sweets than our ration book said. Everything seemed to be rationed in those days so it was a special treat when the occasional 'toffee parcel' arrived for us from Australia. My Cousin Martha had emigrated to the antipodes just after the Second World War and we were very glad she had. The parcel contained all sorts of goodies, but the ones I remember most were the enormous toffee lollies as big as footballs. Australia must have been lollypop ration free and I wanted to go and live there with my Cousin Martha, but nobody seemed to be listening to me, which was usually the way of things.

Gormless Gregory, for reasons unknown, had two sweet ration books which did not seem fair considering he was good at nicking stuff so did not really need two as much as I did. Perhaps he was not so gormless after all. I think maybe it was because his dad limped and they felt sorry for him that they allowed him double rations. He maintained the second book belonged to a cousin of his who had died at birth, but I knew this was just another one of his numerous fabrications.

There were two other sweet shops in our area at that time, the 'Bon-Bon', run by Mrs. Lyons who was also very short but not as short as Mrs. Long. She was a nice old lady who had the patience of Job with us youngsters as we would take an eternity to choose the kind of toffees best suited to the ration coupons available. Occasionally, Mr.

Lyons put in an appearance and always had time to chat to us as we ogled at the treasures on display. He had retired from factory work some years earlier and was idling his time away as best he could. Occasionally he slipped us, unknown to his wife, a bar of nougat or a 'Five Boys' which was a very thin layer of chocolate stamped with the effigy of five boy's faces on the surface of the bar. I am sure he got his reward in heaven.

Behind the counter was a mirror hanging on the wall advertising Fry's Five Boys' Chocolate with faces engraved on the glass and a slogan written underneath each face. Desperation, Pacification, Expectation, Acclamation, and under the last face, Realisation "It's Fry's". Each face showed a different expression reflecting the word written below. All very clever and it fascinated me every time I went in.

The Bon-Bon had a lovely large, mahogany counter which shone. On top of the counter, thick brass rails, also highly polished, held glass panels which prevented the likes of Gormless Gregory from nicking any of the goodies. On the wall next to the mirror was a large clock with the words, 'Nestles Milk For All Time', painted around the face: The tiled floor was scrubbed clean every morning by Mrs. Lyons who was often witnessed carrying out this chore on her hands and knees. It all added to the splendour of this Aladdin's cave where bottles of Bull's Eyes, Coconut Macaroons, Liquorice Torpedoes and Zubes were just some of the delights on display.

To tempt us further, big jars of yellow and pink sherbet sat on the counter waiting to be weighed into small, V shaped, paper bags. This powder discoloured your lips and tongue and made you burp. Outside the shop, a tin board told us, 'It's The Tobacco That Counts', referring to Players Navy Cut cigarettes that could be purchased from within. Gormless said he never smoked Navy Cut because they were too dear but preferred Wild Woodbines that could be bought five at a time in a paper packet. Park Drive and Airman were also sold in fives and Domino singularly, but were not to his liking, he being a connoisseur of such things.

The other sweet shop was run by Mr. and Mrs. Oliver and for some reason was called 'Olivers'. They were not so kind and used to tell our parents everything we got up to. They must have led very shallow lives to be able to spend time spying on us and then 'grassing' to our guardians without a blink of an eyelid. I did not use that shop very much after Mr. Oliver told my mum I had spent all my coupon ration on Victory V lozenges and nothing else. I am not quite sure why this was of such importance as I liked Victory V's and bought them regularly, but nevertheless, on this occasion was reported for doing so. My mum wanted to know why, and it started to take on the significance of a major incident with me in the hot seat. I began to dread going home for fear of her starting again about those blessed lozenges I wished I had never set eyes on! I went off them somewhat after this.

One of the favourite games of the fifties was 'window spotting' which involved the nearby shops. Organised by the local Chamber of Commerce, this kept us out of mischief for hours on end. Participating shops displayed a red disc of about six inches diameter in a prominent place in their shop window. The object of the game was to spot the item in the window not normally sold in that particular shop. For instance, the Bon-Bon placed a baby's rattle amongst its display of sweets and chocolates. Mr. Ashworth, the upholsterer, had a bunch of artificial flowers in a brass vase tucked alongside a settee and Timpson, the shoe shop, put a sweet in its wrapping paper between a pair of shoes. Perfect Outfitters, the supplier of men's elegant suites, for those who could afford them, placed a small nail file on the lapel of one of their finest jackets and it amazed us how it didn't fall off.

So it went on, with dozens of retailers taking part in the fun, except the Olivers who thought the whole thing childish!! Half the problem was being sure you had located all the shops taking part, because if you missed just one, then you were not going to win the prize on offer. An entry form was picked up from any of the shops playing the game and, when completed, handed back for collection and scrutiny by a member of the committee. If you succeeded in spotting all the 'out of place' items, and it was not always easy, your completed form was put into a container and one lucky winner was drawn out. I never knew anyone that won. We always maintained it was one of the kids whose dad was on the committee, but I am sure this was just sour grapes. The winner's prize must have been something special because I can not now remember what it was, but this was not really the issue. Like the Olympic Games, it was not the winning but the taking part that was important.

***

4

Golden Hill Park was our local recreation area, though why it was so called was a total mystery. It was not golden; it was a sort of asphalt colour and had no hills. In fact, it was as flat as my mother's singing but nevertheless it served its purpose as a gathering place for all sorts of activities. Grimshaw's ice cream van would park up at the entrance to this oasis of pleasure to sell us, if we could afford it, the most delicious ice cream the world has ever known. If not, free broken wafer biscuits were very acceptable.

There was an open topped bandstand in the centre of the park that had a little doorway where entrance was gained to the underside of the concrete structure. A locked wooden door had prohibited access but this had been removed at some time and never replaced. It was like an air raid shelter and hours of fun were passed within its dark confines. I heard that Gormless Gregory used it for more dirty activities but that was only hearsay. I do not remember any bands ever performing on it which was a pity really as this was the purpose for which it was built.

The park also had a couple of football pitches used every Saturday during the season by local teams, one run by my dad, taking on opponents from the neighbouring area. These matches, although only amateur and of limited skill, were very well attended and it was not unusual to find a hundred or so people gathered on a match day to cheer on the teams. Of course, this was in the days before mass television, and money was at a premium, so one took one's pleasures and entertainment where one could find them.

The best use of the park, as far as I was concerned, was when the travelling fair took up residence with their many stalls and thrilling rides, the ghost train being my favourite. I found the fairground workers rather scary though, in the same way the gypsies made me feel ill at ease, and I would give them a wide berth when they used the local shops and other amenities. Is it my imagination or were fairs a lot bigger in those days of yore than they are today! Is it because I was smaller then that every ride and side show appeared on a grander scale, or is distance of time distorting the truth!

I recall the boxing booth where the local hard men would line up after a few pints of Dutch courage to take on the champion. I do not remember the local lad ever claiming the £5 on offer to the winner. There were 'rude' tents where you had to be over sixteen to enter, but no fairground worker ever refused my two bob entrance fee, albeit I was only about twelve. Inside these tents, naughty ladies could be seen in the nude but they were not allowed to move at all. It was the law. Bare boobs and bums were on open display but they had better not wobble in the breeze or the local constabulary would be on hand to render summonses.

I won many goldfish and plenty of coconuts on the fair, the coconuts being delicious, especially the milk I found inside by hammering a rusty nail through the eye at the end of the shell to gain entrance. The goldfish never seemed to last for long and were flushed down the lavatory after they became ex-goldfish. There was the rifle range where, if you knocked down five upright metal fingers with an air pellet, you were the proud owner of a bit of tat. However, the odds were stacked against you as the sights of the rifles were always bent off centre which, until you became used to the misalignment, caused you to fire wide. All part of the fun of the fair but a rip off all the same. I was always sad when the time came for them to pack up and move on. But this had its upside as well because we would then scour the area the fairground had occupied in the hope of finding a shilling or two abandoned to its fate. We rarely found anything more than a half eaten toffee apple!

***

None of the people in my neighbourhood went away on summer holidays, that was the privilege of the more affluent members of society and those who lived down south. I knew the Southerners went away because I had seen them on Pathe News at the cinema sunning themselves on the golden sand at Brighton, wherever that might be. No, us Northerners had more important things to do like going to work to keep the country afloat, so the Southerners could go to the beach at Brighton. Therefore, it came as somewhat of a surprise to hear dad say we were to go for a week to Wales.

I was about eleven at the time and, although I thought I was reasonably good at geography, I was not quite sure where Wales was. I had heard of it, of course, because that is where a lot of the Scousers had gone to live during and after the second world war, but as to its location, well, we would see. Dad had booked a week in a chalet at a place called Gronant, which was near Prestatyn I was told. Now I was a whole lot wiser! "Where is Prestatyn?" I asked. "It's in Wales you dumb cluck," our John told me. Well that was O.K. then, at least one of us knew.

Our Daisy said she had a friend who knew of somebody who had gone to Wales on holiday but never came back because they had drowned in the sea somewhere near Rhyl. I had nightmares for a fortnight before our holiday.

A work mate of dad's had a son who owned a car and would be willing, for monetary return, to transport us to and from Gronant. This was arranged and so we all set off in a lovely, big, shiny, Wolsley motor car for the seaside. I had never been so far in a motor car before and it was sheer delight to watch the countryside glide effortlessly by as we headed towards a 'foreign' country. I tried to attract the attention of lesser mortals who had to walk as we drove by but few seemed to be interested in my new found exalted status.

The chalet was located, along with dozens of others, in a place called The Warren, a part of Gronant completely given over to holiday accommodation. It was constructed of timber roughly nailed to make a dwelling of some sorts, painted pale green and had no discernible shape to it. It was a mishmash of rooms that seemed to have come together by accident. Paraffin lamps provided the illumination and water had to be drawn from a communal well about half a mile away.

Nevertheless, the holiday went splendidly with us young ones enjoying the sand dunes whilst mum and dad went for a pint to the nearest local, the Gronant Inn. Some days we were allowed to sit on barrels in the yard of the inn, which nowadays would be called a pub garden, and enjoyed the most delicious Cornish pasties with our lemonade.

The amusement arcade, where I spent most of the pennies I had been given, was great fun and many happy hours slipped by within its glittering interior. The fairground workers on the pleasure beach at nearby Rhyl did not seem so frightening as the ones who had scared the hell out of me on the travelling fairs that visited Golden Hill Park, even though they were just as scruffy and unkempt. I enjoyed the pleasure beach with its ghost train and candy floss, but never went anywhere near the big dipper! The smell of the fried onions on the hot dog stalls was mind boggling and I found it impossible to pass without buying one. Every day was scorching hot and everyone was happy with not a care in the world, or that is how it seemed. I wonder if it was really like that, or do I have a selective memory. Whatever the truth, that was my very first holiday and I will remember it forever.

***

Henry Rex Piers George Sebastian Clements was another pal of mine, but I called him Jim. I cannot remember why, but his mother must have been a bit weird to give him a moniker like that. He had a brother- in- law who played rugby for Salford and Jim thought this fact made him a hard case. He often appeared wearing a rugby skullcap and pranced around like a scrum half until somebody planted him right between the eyes with a straight left and the scull cap was never seen again.

Jim was a beautiful sketcher and quite an authority on birds, that is the feathered type, and knew every 'make' there was. His many drawings of wild birds would regularly be pinned up on the school notice board. Sickening it was. The only time I had any mention on the notice board was when I was required to see the Headmaster. Terrifying was how I would describe the feeling of being summoned to the Head's study. Later in life as a Prison Officer, I faced many prison rioters but never managed to achieve that feeling of distress a call to 'Beak's' office produced .

Gordon Whitehouse, our headmaster, was a football referee on the FIFA list who had officiated in many international matches and was known worldwide. More importantly, he knew my dad. Any misdemeanour committed by me went straight back home, which I felt was unfair. Other boys could commit murder and get away with it, but all my transgressions were reportable red card offences. The common ground between Mr. Whitehouse and my dad was, of course, football. Dad had been a fair player himself and my Uncle Joe played professionally for Everton, until he was caught with the manager's wife, but that is another story.

Dad was now doing a good job coaching a local amateur side who worked out of the British Legion. He used to take my elder brothers and several other youths from the area onto Golden Hill Park and instruct them in the finer arts of the game. I, of course, had to stand and watch, not being allowed to join in for reasons that I never knew and still do not. I was allowed to retrieve the ball when it left the designated playing area and return it to the privileged ones who were benefiting from this latter day Svengali, my dad. This was despite the fact that I was a reasonable player myself and was a current member of the school team.

My football boots were those our John had outgrown but I did not mind because they kept my feet dry. They did not have holes in the soles like my only pair of shoes. I used to cut innersoles out of cardboard, usually Shredded Wheat boxes, and place them inside to help keep out the cold and the occasional pebble that decided to hitch a ride embedded under my foot. The cardboard was not very waterproof and only lasted a short time before reinforcement was called for. We could not afford to buy shoes very often so the holes had to be pretty big before replacements were provided. The holes which appeared underneath my socks matched the ones my big toes poked through, so no problem there. When the toe holes got too large I would pull the sock down and fold the front part under my foot. It meant the top of my sock got smaller and smaller but that was not important.

My brother John was probably a better footballer than I and played for his school team. Being four years older than me he was quite naturally in the higher school. Dad never missed one of his matches, yet never attended any I played in. That is the way it was. I got used to it and the hurt abated and in the end I stopped telling him when and where we were playing.

Mr. Chapples came to notice I was the best goalkeeper since the great Frank Swift and so appointed me as the school goalie. At our school in those days only the ten 'out' players' shirts were provided, because naturally they had to be the school colours. The goalie had to provide his own. I only had one jumper and that had to do for school in the winter, so I asked my mother if she would buy me one. "Don't talk bloody daft lad," I was told, "Go and ask Mrs Nunn next door if her Colin has got any old ones he doesn't want." Colin was her only son and a member of our gang, better known to us as 'Skiver' and was spoiled rotten.

I duly trotted off next door feeling like an uninvited refugee. I did not like going next door because they had a little Jack Russell called Bosun that took great delight in biting kids' bums. I somehow managed to dodge this vicious little bitch and found Mrs Nunn very accommodating. She produced the most awful looking piece of clothing it has ever been my misfortune to clap eyes on. It was a brownish coloured, hand knitted woollen sweater that had come adrift at the neck and had tentacles of wool hanging down the front. I showed it to our centre half who said it was not even good enough to throw away. Good enough or not it lasted me three seasons and managed to save many penalties.

I must admit though that it did cause me embarrassment on occasions, especially when I saw the lovely clean, green, roll neck pullies that some of the goalies wore. I was the only goalkeeper in the entire school league that didn't wear green. That brown jumper never did get washed for fear of it falling to pieces. Mother maintained that it would only get dirty again playing on all those muddy pitches so what was the point? The mud could easily be scraped off with a stick or knife when it dried.

One school match was played in Stretford in such appalling conditions I do not know to this day who won the game. The fog was so thick the game should never have kicked off, but we were not playing under FIFA rules, we were playing under Mr. Chapples' rules, and he said we played. I was in goal as usual and only set eyes on the ball when it entered our own six yard area and then it was too late to do much about it. I do not know how the opposition knew where our goal was, or how our team knew where theirs was. All one could hear was shouting coming out of the gloom. I knew that January morning what it felt like to have cataracts. It went so quiet at one stage I thought everyone had gone home and left me, but found this was not the case when the ball appeared from nowhere and hit me in the face, much to the amusement of those close enough to witness the incident. There was a dispute over the final score, Victoria Park claiming they had won seven five, and our team claiming victory by the same score. Mr.

Chapples was referee that day and claimed he had not a clue who had scored what.

***

On Bank Road next to the tennis courts was a huge house whose garden backed onto Albert Park. The garden was actually an orchard and hidden from the park by a bandstand, fashioned after the Hollywood Bowl. John O'Sullivan was a pal of mine and fellow gang member from down our entry. Together we decided there were too many apples and pears on the trees. So many, in fact, the trees were in danger of collapse with all the weight and it would be kindness itself if we relieved them of some of their burden.

The way into the orchard was over a restrictive high wire fence some untrusting sole had erected all around the ground. How could they be so treacherous as to think people might want to gain access to their property! It was not the Christian way of looking at things and they would have to be taught a lesson. John and I were just the ones to do it. It took some scaling but we managed it somehow, even though I fell from the top of the wire and disturbed a bevy of bees who were enjoying a rotten apple laying on the ground. Our entrance resembled a couple of British prisoners escaping from Stalag Luft 111, the only difference being they were getting out and we were getting in.

Once inside, the darkness of the orchard took us by surprise. The vast number of trees blocked out the light and gave the place an atmosphere of foreboding. What if they had a dog! Would it bite us! What if they had a gardener! The questions came thick and fast and I cursed John for talking me into this venture. He said it was the other way round and I had talked him into it. It was unusual for John to tell lies, him being a good Catholic and that, but I let it pass. Seeing as we were here we might as well help ourselves to the bounty on offer and started to fill our jumpers with the fruit that looked and smelled delicious. The smell reminded me of the empty fruit boxes Shilton's greengrocers threw into the entry for our removal.

With our jumpers full to overflowing it was impossible to climb the wire fence to make good our escape. I said to John he should have foreseen this situation and made contingency plans. He said it was my fault for telling him the orchard was there in the first place. I said he was telling lies again as he had always known about the orchard and would have to spend all Saturday morning at the confessional with Father Riprap who didn't much care for apple thieves.

The solution was for one of us to climb the wire to the outside and receive the spoils that could be passed through or over the fence by the one still in the orchard. The only question was who would go and who would stay. John said he should go first and receive the fruit because, if I went first and somebody came, I would run off and leave him in the orchard to face the death penalty on his own. I asked how he could have such a low opinion of me and he said through experience. I said I should go first because I was the youngest by two months and a Protestant and this was a Protestant country, with muttered reference to King Henry *VIII*. He would have none of this, saying that the Catholics had just as much right to live here as the Protestants, and that we should toss a coin to decide. Neither of us had any money. We settled the matter by deciding whoever could eat a pear the fastest would climb out first. John won because he was two months older than me so, therefore, had a bigger mouth.

Both safely on the outside, jumpers and pockets stuffed with apples and pears and feeling extremely smug, we made our way out of the park and into the path of a policeman who just happened to be walking by, as they did in those days. An added problem arose here because every policeman outside of the Metropolitan Police District knew my dad, or said they did, and this one was no exception. He 'escorted' us to the front of the house to which the orchard belonged by means of holding my left ear and John's right. His knock on the door was answered by a maid in a black pinafore and little black thing on her head which made John and me laugh. I had never seen the likes before but the copper must have thought we were laughing at something else and clipped our ears. She said she would have to call the master and disappeared into the gloom of the house.

Our laughter quickly turned to horror on recognising the 'master' as Mr. Bentley, our science teacher at school. He produced a couple of bags for us to place our swag in, thanked us for saving him the job of collecting the fruit himself, gave us one apple each and sent us on our way. He showed his gratitude to the policeman by inviting him inside for a cup of tea, bid us farewell and closed the door. *Phew*! He had not recognised us. To add insult to injury, the apple he gave us tasted sour.

During my next science lesson Mr. Bentley came to me

and said my face was familiar and did I not owe him some homework or something. I said he must have mistaken me for somebody else, possibly John O'Sullivan. He said it would come to him in due course as my face definitely rang a bell but he could not for the moment think why. Thankfully he never did.

***

5

One hot summer when we were on those dear halcyon school holidays; (funny how the summers were always hot and lasted forever when one was young), Don, another pal of mine and gang member from down the entry, Skiver and me built a canoe from old orange boxes thrown out of the back door of Shilton's greengrocers. We covered the frame work with old material Skiver's mother had produced from somewhere, (that woman seemed able to provide anything that was asked for) and nailed it together with tacks we managed to prise out of the lino in our respective kitchens. Not too many tacks you understand, just enough to ensure their disappearance would not be readily noticed. A spade would serve as a paddle.

This 'state of the art' craft, Camel Laird would have been proud to announce as one of theirs, was ceremonially carried around Upshaw to show the wide eyed public how clever we were. We must have impressed them because many heads turned in our direction and mumbling could be heard coming from mums out shopping. They were obviously wishing their sons could have played a part in such a creative venture as the one they had just had the privilege of clapping eyes on!

Our next destination after the grand 'get a load of this' parade was to the meadows, a lush green area that was countryside to us. The River Mersey ran through the meadows on its way to Liverpool and was a magnet to the kids of the area. You could swim, paddle, throw stones at the rats or float canoes down there without the intervention of grown ups who had tiresome ideas of saving you from drowning or catching the bubonic plague. They always had to spoil the fun. Gormless Gregory maintained that he had gone down there alone one night and had drowned, but had come back to life again. We never really believed him though.

The grand launch was about to take place and had attracted a legion of urchins from all over the meadows. The look of envy and resentment was written all over their faces. How they wished they could be party to this great adventure that could lead to a Nobel Prize for inventiveness. The painstaking hours of design and hard labour all seemed worthwhile as we lowered our exquisite craft into the rippling stream that was the Mersey. Whilst we thought it was a rippling stream, it was, in fact, a raging torrent. But we were intrepid.

Skiver said he should be first into the boat because his mum had supplied the material to cover it and we found it hard to reason against this logic. In stepped Skiver with Don and I holding on to the little boat for all we were worth. That should have been a warning to us, but as I have said we were intrepid. The boat suddenly turned turtle and out shot the surprised Skiver into the saturated deluge amid a tirade of foul and abusive language. The craft sped off down stream to be smashed against the first set of obstacles it found then disappeared out of sight, no doubt finishing up at New Brighton on the Wirral. All that work, hardship and sleepless nights wondering if we would reach Australia were gone.

Skiver, drenched to the skin and his ego dented beyond repair after his fall from grace in front of all those kids, who turned out not to be so envious after all, blamed it on Don and me. If we had held on tighter he would have been O.K., he maintained. The fact that the material his mother had provided had not taken the weight we had burdened it with, was thought about but never mentioned.

***

The meadows helped to pass many a summer afternoon but not all of it was pleasurable and carefree. Mother had taken my sister Daisy, brothers Neil and John and myself along with some of the scruffs from our back entry for a picnic there one hot afternoon. This was one family outing in which I was included. Part of the picnic fare was made up with those bottles of concentrated orange juice we received free from the state along with bottles of cod liver oil and malt. The orange juice we watered down to make a delicious fruit drink but the rest was not so impressive and usually ended up in the dustbin. The Government thought we needed such items because food was still pretty much in short supply after the great conflict, and we required the vitamins to make us big and strong, so we could fight the Germans again if they tried their luck for a third time. Dad was in the Legion after finishing the early shift in the steelworks and would join us when he had had his fill of Guinness.

The afternoon was going along nicely. Dad had joined us and immediately fallen asleep on the banks of the river in which we young ones were playing. Neil, the eldest of the four of us, was a little above playing games and was stretched out on the top of the riverbank pretending to be an adult. Daisy was swimming in the Mersey, which was clean in those days and free from the sewage that would pollute it and kill its wild life in later years.

Suddenly, screams were heard and we looked on helplessly as Daisy was being tossed and turned around in a whirlpool that had appeared from nowhere. Mum dashed into the water up to her waist, but being unable to swim and of a somewhat rotund stature was getting into difficulties. As much as we screamed and shouted dad could not be aroused. The Guinness had taken a good grip on him and he slumbered on in complete ignorance of the drama unfolding before his unopened eyes.

Neil had suddenly awakened from his daydreaming about Diana Dors or whatever, and quickly established if he did not act quickly both Daisy and mother would be lost in the flow of the river. Up he jumped and took a running dive from the top of the bank on which he had been fantasising straight into the gushing maelstrom that seemed to be increasing its haste even as we watched. Tarzan had nothing on our Neil.

Just when we thought Daisy must be a 'gonna' Neil reached her and, doing his life saving stroke, brought her to the bank where we quickly dragged her ashore amongst much gasping and sobbing. Then, from out of nowhere, he re-appeared with mother safely in tow. All were well and safe but it had been a harrowing experience for all of us, except dad who could not make out what all the fuss was about when we eventually managed to waken him from his state of deep unconsciousness. The severe beating he took about the head and shoulders from mother helped him in this respect.

***

Bluebell Woods was about six miles from Upshaw, a fact that never stopped us trekking down Folton Road, passed Shell Chemicals and into the wide open space that was called Haldingham in those days. The woods have now totally disappeared into the great forest beyond to be substituted by a conglomerate of dwelling houses. Country lanes and footpaths have long since been replaced by tarmac roads and industrial estates but back then, tranquillity reigned. The walk to Bluebell Woods was half the pleasure, the other half being the forest itself. The country lanes were full of the sounds of songbirds with dragon flies hovering like brightly coloured gossamer in the balmy summer breeze. Here I could escape from the everyday drudge of bookie running and baby minding into a world of Robin Hood and the Sheriff of Nottingham. This was my Sherwood. The woods presented a dark mysterious ambience that never failed to hold my imagination and many pleasant hours were passed in its shady interior.

The enchantment of the woods was something that captured both Don and Skiver as well as myself and we spent ages exploring for treasure we felt sure had been hidden there by the Crusaders returning from the holy wars. We never found any but maybe we did not look in the right places. I felt certain if we could only get into the woodman's hut we would find it full of gold and jewels worth a king's ransom. But it was always securely locked so imagine our surprise one day when we ventured into Sherwood to find it open.

We peeked inside and found the place bereft of treasure but full of uninteresting things like mugs, old lemonade bottles and magazines with pictures of trees on the covers. There were balls of string, saws, hammers, axes and wooden stakes, presumably for sticking through the heart of any vampire foolish enough to trespass in the woods. An old table, tatty armchair and a cupboard were the only furniture on show. A Primus stove sat on the table with a kettle perched on top. There were all kinds of other oddments lying about, but they meant nothing to us and appeared singularly boring.

After prying for a while into something that was none of our business, I asked, "Why do you think it is open this time when all other times we have been here it has been locked up?" On getting no reply, I looked around to find I was alone. Panic took hold of me because through the open doorway I could see a man making his way towards the hut. He was about fifty yards away yet I could hear the rustle of the undergrowth as he made his way between the trees and ferns. *Blimey!*, what do I do now! Hide behind the chair! Crouch under the table! No, that was no good he was bound to see me. The hut was windowless so no escape that way.

He was getting nearer and whistling a tuneless refrain just like Skiver did all the time. I wondered if he might be an uncle of Skivers seeing as he knew the same discordant melody, but remembered Skiver had told me he had no uncles when I told him about my Uncle Joe. Frozen with terror, I stood and awaited the arrival of what must be the woodman. I closed my eyes thinking he would not be able to see me if I did that. After what seemed an eternity, with my heart beating like mad, I felt a tap on my arm and thought, "This is it. I'm dead." I had to open my eyes sometime so it might as well be now. When I did, Don was standing there with a stupid grin on his face. "It's O.K.," he said, "He's gone straight on by." "You rotter," I balled at him, "Where did you both vanish to?" He explained that Skiver and he had heard someone approaching and, not being very brave, decided to scarper before they got caught. They had tried to warn me but did not dare make a noise for fear of being taken prisoner.

Funny how some lads like to play the goody and some

the baddy. Don and Skiver were consistently on the side of the angels whilst I was always the villain, the one with the black hat, meaning the odds were stacked in their favour being two on to one. We made swords and shields out of wood, which we took with us to re-enact the holy wars of the crusaders. Don and Skiver had a red cross crayoned on their shield to denote they were goodies. Many a battle was fought in the depth of the greenwood but I always lost because two swords are better than one. Hide and seek in the woods was great fun as long as you did not lose yourself, which we managed to do on several occasions. However, that was part of the fun and excitement and we never stayed lost for long.

Gormless Gregory came with us only once, but found it altogether too frightening for his liking and steered clear of any further expeditions in that direction. It was possibly all the talk of being eaten alive by wolves who inhabited such places that had put him off treasure hunting amongst the woodland. We tried to reassure him that the wolves were friendly really and only wanted to play but he would have none of it.

Nothing would keep us from going there and it rained so hard on one of our sorties that by the time we got home our clothing was stuck to our bodies and had to be peeled off us like banana skins. But it was worth every discomfort imaginable to be amid the freshness of that beautiful wood which sadly no longer exists.

***

6

Being a member of a Liverpool family who moved to Upshaw during world war two to escape the Luftwaffe's bombardment of the Merseyside docks, it is not surprising I spent periods of my childhood in Liverpool , staying with my aunties and uncles. Auntie Beattie was my favourite as she was a real tomboy who whistled continuously, enjoyed playing football and rounders and had a wicked sense of humour. I thought she was quite beautiful. She had played football for Dick - Kerr's Ladies, probably the most famous ladies' team of the period. They were formed in 1917 by the Lancashire firm of W.B. Dick and John Kerr, makers of tramway and light railway equipment. Women were employed in this factory during the first world war producing ammunition and had taken to playing football with the lads during their tea breaks. The legend of Dick - Kerr's Ladies started right there in the works' yard and would remain in existence for forty eight years.

Ladies' football was frowned upon in those days and was not recognised by the F.A. It was considered unsuitable for the female anatomy and ought not to be encouraged.

Anyway, in those black and white days women were supposed to know their place, and that was in the home, not playing football with the men folk. It would remain ostracised until the late 1960's or early 1970's when the Football Association finally condescended and allowed ladies teams to join their illustrious ranks. Although I never saw Auntie Beattie play in a serious game, I often witnessed her prowess with a football and considered her heading ability as second to none. This non-acceptance of ladies' soccer, by the 'powers that be', fitted in nicely with her rebellious character and made her all the more determined to play the game she loved. However, giving birth to two babies in quick succession put paid to her playing career.

Auntie Beattie was my godmother and on her sideboard was a photograph of herself in air force uniform holding me dressed in a white frock at my Christening. *What a thought!* Underneath her right foot was a football. She had been in the air force during the war and had married an airman who paid the ultimate price. However, she was now happily married to a super guy named Peter who, amongst other things, was a very good artist. His painted murals on the landing walls of their house were a sight to behold and held me spellbound.

One of the biggest treats when visiting Liverpool was a ride on the overhead railway. It ran along the whole length of the docks from Dingle in the south to Seaforth and Litherland in the north. The structure was a continuous bridge of steel framework and decking, inspired by the New York elevated railway. Built in the 1890's, it was a masterpiece of engineering and was known as 'The

Docker's Umbrella'. It was an electric track, steam being considered too dangerous with the numerous flammable cargoes that could be ignited by the locomotive's sparks. However, a steam powered line ran underneath the elevated track for much of its length and this served the Liverpool Docks, which rather contradicted the reason for the elevated track being electric. There were other advantages, of course, for electrification, such as speed, cleanliness, quiet running and, not least, being more economical. Coming down the steps from the overhead railway, it was not unusual to have a freight train pass right in front of you running along the street on its way to or from one of the many busy docks operating at that time.

An elevated railway had been proposed as early as 1852 but had never been acted upon. The Mersey Docks and Harbour Board had to find a way of easing congestion along the many miles of dockland but had met with objections at every turn. By 1888, the problems had become critical and something needed to be done as a matter of urgency. A party of eminent businessmen got together and formed the Liverpool Overhead Railway Company and obtained the Dock Board's permission to start building. Sir Douglas Fox and Freddie Henry Greathead, two of the leading engineers of the day, got their heads and pencils together and set to work on designing the railway. Construction began in October 1889 and was completed in January 1893. It was formally opened the following month by the Marquis of Salisbury.

The view obtained from the Overhead Railway really was superb. One could see the towns of the Wirral across the water and, on a clear day, as far as the Welsh

Mountains. Nearer at hand were the docks themselves, very active at that time, with many ocean going liners tied up alongside the Pier Head. On one occasion I saw an enormous liner with three yellow funnels laying at berth and was told it was the S.S. Rena del Mar, or some such name, a ship my dad had sailed on many times to South America. He did not see a lot of the ocean however, because he spent most of his time stuck below decks in the boiler room, stoking away.

The thing I found most fascinating and, indeed, baffling, was the fact that the overhead railway entered a subterranean tunnel at the southern terminal, that is, at Dingle. The train went over a lattice girder bridge and into the bowels of the earth. One then had to climb a flight of stairs to gain access to Park Street and out into the fresh air.

The thought of this still leaves me bewildered and I often wonder if my memory has played an unkind trick on me.

One of the most abiding memories of my rides along the railway was the sight of men massed in bunches outside public houses awaiting opening time. We passed many of these on our aerial sojourns along the waterfront, they being clearly visible on the many back streets. It was not unusual to see as many as two dozen men braving the elements, waiting for the landlord to unbolt the gateway to happiness and oblivion. There were so many unemployed at the time I suppose their only solace was in drink, though who suffered in the consequence is a matter of conjecture.

The Overhead Railway closed down in December 1956 due to financial reasons and despite strenuous efforts to find a backer, none could be found. Rigorous public protests could do nothing to save the line, and so, alas, it died. The flat fronted, wooden framed, rolling stock would be seen no more. On its closure, H. Maxwell Roston, the General Manager of Liverpool Overhead Railway said, "The time will come when Merseysiders must rue the day when they permitted the City Fathers to throttle the lifeblood of this unique undertaking and, in addition, to scrap the last vestige of their remarkable efficient tramway system."

***

Upshaw swimming pool, known locally as 'The Baths', was a splendid piece of Victoriana and used to the utmost by people from near and far. Many a time I queued outside, waiting to get into one of the most popular leisure centres in the area, only to find when I eventually reached the changing room, no lockers were available. In those days it was perfectly safe to leave ones clothing and towel in a bundle by the side of the attendant's room, not that anyone would want to nick my gear anyway. The pool was quite frequently packed to and over capacity, which I am sure nowadays would not be permitted for safety reasons, but I do not remember anything untoward ever happening. The building had a huge glass dome that glistened in the sunlight and resembled something seen in Raj controlled India. The whole building was clean and bright and the green and white tiled interior added to its splendour.

School galas and swimming lessons were held there on a regular basis. The best times, however, were had in the summer holidays, when it was too hot to do anything else but lounge around in the cool water, and splash the many people who had paid tuppence to watch. Whole families would go *en bloc* and take a picnic with them to be enjoyed after the bathing had finished. Hours of fun were to be had whilst the shrill sound of the lifeguard's whistle echoed around the rotunda, to be mostly ignored by all and sundry.

For a period in the 1950s we were not allowed anywhere near the place because of the outbreak of infantile paralysis, or poliomyelitis as it is now known, an acute infectious viral disease especially affecting children. It attacks the brain and the spinal chord causing weakness and paralysis which, in turn, leads to wasting of muscle. It scared the living daylights out of us, because we were told it was spread by loads of kids bathing together, and we had been doing this for ages. My mate Jim did actually catch the disease and for a long time it was touch and go whether he would fully recover, but thankfully he made it through.

The building had a dual role insomuch as it was transformed into a ballroom in the winter months. This was achieved by placing wooden boards across the length and breadth of the pool, no mean feat considering its shape. It had a bulbous centre approximately thirty feet across and a length of one hundred feet. I never witnessed this transformation but have often wondered how it was done.

Alas, this magnificent building had to be taken down. It had fallen into disrepair over the years through wanton or constructive neglect; I know not which but I have my suspicions. A sad affair, but something that has become commonplace. The site was turned into a housing complex. People need houses and houses mean money and money talks.

***

Christmas was always special and not only for the presents we received but for the general atmosphere that surrounded the whole festive season. The stories we were told at school about the three wise men coming from the east with gifts for baby Jesus, and the shepherds tending their sheep in the fields were magic to the ears of us young ones, even though it was a load of old claptrap. The baby laying with a herd of cattle in a barn always struck me as being somewhat unhygienic and a thing his dad should not have allowed, but allow it he did so that was that.

Wassailing, a thing that one seldom sees or hears nowadays but was commonplace in my youth, helped to spread the feeling of wellbeing and light-hearted merriment. Wassailing, the practice of going to people's front doors and singing Christmas Carols, often in an untutored, tuneless and 'offensive to the ears' manner that never seemed to upset anyone, was good clean fun. These sing songs were, in the main, arranged by the local churches, and choristers would stand outside pubs and hotels to collect funds for the various activities they engaged in. A member of the Baptist Church Choir knocked on our front door one year and started singing carols with her mates. The choir was mostly young women who sang away to their hearts' delight until I told them our John was not in and they quickly set off to wassail elsewhere.

Mum always made her own Christmas pudding, usually months before the event, and hung it up on the clothes rack dangling from the ceiling in the kitchen. She placed silver thrupenny bits in the pudding, one for each of us to find on Christmas day. The coins were only small and how we did not choke to death on them is something short of a miracle. However, the thrill of finding a silver thrupence was worth the risk of death by asphyxiation and was enjoyed by us all. We thought it was very clever the way the coins managed, seemingly unaided, to find themselves one on each plate. *Mum's trickery knew no bounds.*

Christmas was celebrated big style in our house even though we were far from religious. In fact, I did not know Christmas had anything to do with religion for the first umpteen years of my life, and looking at it today I am still not so sure that it has. Commercialism did not have such a hold back then, because money was scarce, but we still managed our annual pilgrimage into Manchester to visit the big stores like Lewis's, Pauldens and Woolworth's.

Selecting which comic annual to have was always a special delight, and a visit to Santa's Grotto was a treat we looked forward to every year. That is till I recognised my Uncle Joe Isherwood was Santa. My confusion was profound, because although I knew Father Christmas could not be in all the big stores at once, I thought his brothers helped him out. But this was not the real Santa or even one of his brothers, it was Uncle Joe. Not the Uncle Joe who had played for Everton, that would not have been so bad, but another Uncle Joe who hated kids. In my childish mind confusion reigned.

Nevertheless, the Christmas parties went down a treat, with us young ones attending several different ones. This was due to dad joining various clubs just before Yuletide to get our names on the list. We were always given good presents at these parties because the clubs tried to outdo each other with the standard of gift they gave. Pantomime and the circus trips also came courtesy of dad's clubs at this time of year and were looked forward to with great delight. In later years, many a teenage love affair began on such outings, although these never amounted to much nor lasted very long.

Uncle Joe was sacked by Lewis's after his second year as Santa because they said he scared too many kids.

***

7

Eli was a genuine ninny. He appeared from time to time down our back entry but lord knows where he came from. Don thought he lived somewhere off Lower Road, which was on the other side of Upshaw Bridge and somewhat foreign territory to us, but we never did find out exactly where. He always wore one of those hats that covered the whole of the head, a little like the old fashioned pilot's helmet but not as elegant, and this made him look like a fly. So Eli became 'the fly'. He had a brother called Cedric. Now can you imagine Eli and Cedric in the same family, their mother deserved her backside kicking for lumbering the world with these two. Cedric was a bit older than Eli but just as dumb and had a hair lip that made him the brunt of many a joke. Poor lad was as big a goof as his brother and the pair of them spent their entire school life in the gardening class. I seem to recall another brother called Septimus, but thankfully I never got to meet him.

Eli said he wanted to become a member of our gang which comprised of Don, Skiver, Gregory, John and Rory O'Sullivan and Len and Barry Jackson, as well as myself.

Gormless Gregory said Eli was too ignorant and brainless to be one of us, which was a bit rich really coming from him. Gregory avowed he had heard that the rival Dodsworth gang were always looking for fresh blood. This, of course, was a lie. The only blood the Dodsworths were looking for was ours, but Eli said he did not like the Dodsworths and we always had a better bonfire than they did. Cedric never said much at all, just stood there looking stupid. God, their dad must have been so proud to have sired such luminous examples of modern youth. They could have stepped straight out of the Bash Street Kids in the Beano, or was it the Dandy, I forget.

The fly always had a runny nose and had that disgusting habit of eating the snail creeping down his top lip. This churned my stomach and I usually took evasive action if I saw him coming down the entry. Somebody suggested we allow him into our gang then use him as Guy Fawkes on bonfire night, but the more sensible ones pointed out that this would be noticed and we would be stopped from doing it. I personally thought the idea was brilliant and perhaps we could make use of their Cedric in the same way.

We gave Gregory the job of getting rid of 'Einstein' and 'Socrates' as they were becoming a bit of an embarrassment to us, and our street credibility would have been zero if the Dodsworth gang found out we were cavorting with such nitwits. Gregory was a well known idiot to everyone including the Dodsworths but at least he was our idiot by way of living down our entry, so we could get away with that one. To import lunacy was not something we were prepared to handle. Whatever Gormless told the brothers, and it was not always prudent to know the way he operated, it seemed to work and we only came across them on rare occasions after that, and then from a distance.

The O'Sullivans were strict Roman Catholic and never missed Sunday mass or holy days of obligation. This, at times was a bit of a bind especially if bonfire wood needed to be nicked, as one had to strike whilst the iron was hot, and both John and Rory were handy lads. Mr. O'Sullivan was an Irishman who worked at the steelworks alongside my dad, and did the same ungodly shift pattern. When either my dad or Mr. O'Sullivan were on nights the noise from the entry during the day had to be kept to a minimum or we would know about it, as the men-folk needed their sleep. Mrs O'Sullivan was English and a convert to the Roman church, which by definition made her more devout than her husband, and as I mentioned earlier, attended holy mass every morning of the week at an hour fit only for owls, pussy cats, burglars and policemen. She was a lovely woman, big in stature and very much the homemaker. For some unknown reason, my mother, who was a great friend of hers, never called her by anything else but her surname, which was accepted without a second thought.

The Jacksons moved into the house next door to the O'Sullivans when I was about ten. Before then two sisters, married to two bizarre geezers who put the willies up me, had occupied the house. One of them worked for the Post Office in some capacity or other and rode a huge bicycle all over the place. The other did not appear to work anywhere at all. He spent a lot of his time peeping through the garden fence to see what we youngsters were doing and I called him Dr. Crippen, after that other creepy character whose effigy I had seen in Louis Tussaud's Waxworks in Blackpool. I was glad when they moved because the Jacksons were lovely people and always made me feel welcome whenever I called. I never set eyes on the father the whole time I knew the family. I think he worked permanent nights, which would seem like a sensible thing to do if you have fifteen kids. Everyone said Len looked like Elvis and I suppose in a way he did, but one thing was for certain, Elvis could sing, Len could not. He tried it once in our front room and my mum pitched us both into the street with the threat that she would call the police if there was any more of it.

One occasion concerning the gang, 'though only as spectators, apart from Skiver who took the Oscar for best supporting actor, is worthy of note. Skiver, was being given a rough time by our John for some

peccadillo he had committed and this led to the former receiving a fat lip. Mr. Nunn, witnessing this incident, decided to administer some justice of his own by clouting our John's ear and pushing him down the entry. I thought this was a bit much. Kids should be able to fight their own battles without the intervention of grown ups, even though our John was four years older than Skiver and outweighed him by about two stones. I decided mum should know, so set off to find her.

She was in the kitchen picking the winners out of the racing page of the Daily Dispatch, winners that usually turned out to be losers, but no matter, this was serious business. I thought hard before interrupting her but decided there was no choice, so jumped in with both feet. I told her Mr. Nunn was just about to string our John up on the gas light that stood at the end of the entry. Those gas lamp standards had nice cross members near the top, just right for lynching miscreants. Thinking it best to go overboard a bit, I had exaggerated the situation because interrupting the selection of race winners was not to be taken lightly. After cursing the holy family thrice, mum jumped up, grabbed the nearest weapon she could lay her hands on, which happened to be a poker laying near the grate, and dashed outside in her pinafore and slippers. I followed not wanting to miss any of the fun.

John was just entering our garden gate with Skiver's dad in close pursuit. Mr. Nunn came to a sudden halt on seeing mum, uttered a word we young ones should never have heard and ran full pelt down the entry with mum close behind. All the gang appeared from nowhere and joined in the procession heading towards Upshaw Bridge. I will never know to this day why Mr. Nunn did not go into his own house but he did not. He headed down Station Road, in the direction of the meadows, with mum shouting obscenities and waving the poker about in a menacing fashion, still in her pinny and slippers.

The gang brought up the rear and thought it great fun but did not get too close for fear of being accidentally struck with a blunt instrument. More kids joined the cavalcade until a great mass were following the two of them and goading my mum to give the big bully a good hiding. She was losing ground on him because he was a lot younger, fitter and certainly slimmer then she was, but still not brave enough to stand and face her. It was like a scene out of the Keystone Cops and had to be seen to be believed.

The entourage entered the meadows and meandered its way along the banks of the River Mersey with mum still screaming what she was going to do to him when she caught him. "Anyone who lays a finger on one of mine has me to answer to," she yelled. Where she got the energy to carry on with this chase I do not know, but carry on she did until she caught him as he got stuck trying to get over a stile that led to freedom across Folton meadows. His arms and shoulders were beaten unmercifully with the poker mum was still carrying in her hand, much to the amusement of the followers, who had faithfully stayed behind her for the two and a half miles or so it had taken her to catch him. She cursed him from pillow to post for attacking a young one. A bit rich I thought, but the thought remained just that! We all then scattered in different directions before mum's wrath descended on us for disobeying earlier instructions to return home and leave her to her business.

No legal proceedings ever followed this assault but I do know Mr. Nunn never hit our John again, or anyone else as far as I am aware.

***

Uncle Joe, he of Everton fame, came to live with us in Upshaw for a short period of time. Not only was he a good footballer, he was also pretty good at almost anything a bit dodgy. Football players did not earn the vast fortunes present day participants enjoy, so Joe earned a bit on the side by helping out with 'surplus' stock from Liverpool docks. This brought him into contact with all shades of characters who would cut your throat for looking at them sideways.

He had crossed some wacko on Merseyside and decided that prudence was the order of the day. A residential address some thirty odd miles east would do very nicely and I had the distinction of having a professional footballer living under the same roof. My street credibility tripled. It would have quadrupled had Uncle Joe played for Manchester United or Manchester City, but you can not have everything.

On Thursday mornings Joe would leave for Liverpool on the 'working men's special' that left Upshaw railway station at 7.10 am. It was cheaper on the special but it stopped at every two-bit halt between Manchester and Liverpool Central and took an eternity. All the Everton players had to report to Goodison Park to get in shape for Saturday's game.

Mum always gave Joe her football pools coupon to post in Liverpool whenever he went, though what was so special about it being posted in 'Scouseland' was another mystery to me. Life was full of mysteries. One Saturday evening dad was checking the football results when all hell broke loose. I disappeared into the cellar in case it was something I had done wrong, and hid behind the pile of coal that lay waiting to be fed to the hungry fire grate in the kitchen.

Mrs Nunn came in, Mrs O'Sullivan came in, Mrs

Jackson came in, the entire population of the world came in. Mum had won first dividend - £75,000, worth millions by today's reckoning. That night a big party was held in the Legion with everyone getting plastered. All the grown-ups that is, we juniors were told our party would come later on.

Joe always stayed in Liverpool until Monday morning when he would catch the special coming the other way. On his arrival he was greeted by mum who flung her arms around his neck and told him her good news.

He went very pale and produced the un-posted pools coupon from his trench coat pocket. His return to Liverpool was swift and he ceased to be a lodger at our house from that moment on. Oh how life could have been so different, and we never did get our party.

***

8

Our local library was a one storey concrete shed that stood in the shadows at the side of Golden Hill Park. It reposed in permanent twilight and had a narrow passageway running along its side that was bush lined and foreboding. This passageway was the scene of many an ambush on the way to and from school by rival gangs of the neighbourhood. The rougher kids of the area, namely the 'Dodsworth Mob', who lacked our refinement and gentility, lived at the other end of this passageway. This gave them the idea they had the right to veto whoever went along its confines. All other kids in the area hotly disputed this claim and many a skirmish took place to settle the right of access and passage. The dispute was a bit like the situation in the Middle East with no obvious solution being available.

The passageway I could handle, the library was not so easy. I decided that I would become a member because I liked the smell of books, at least the ones we had at school. The smell of the books our Daisy had in her bedroom had a somewhat different aroma, something resembling lamb stew. I was told I needed to get my parents' permission to join and required them to sign a form stating I was an upstanding member of the community and would pay for any loss or damage incurred. This I did not think was a very good idea because where money was concerned my mother had strict rules, and these did not include giving money to concrete libraries.

No; there had to be another way. Someone had to forge my mother's signature. It could not be Gormless Gregory because he could not write; Skiver was too clean living and Don's mother would have killed him had she found out, and she would have found out because he told her everything. I could not do it because I was too honest, and anyway they would have recognised my handwriting. Dick Head Dennis was the obvious choice and he would only charge me a Wagon Wheel or a pack of Love Hearts for the service. Dennis duly signed, the fee was paid and I was the proud owner of a library ticket, but I had not reckoned with the librarians.

Two rather elderly, spindly spinsters, who wore pince-nez and had their hair pinned back in a bun, held this lofty position. One look at either of those two was enough to turn one pale and the two together was more than should be asked of anyone. The ugly sisters in the annual pantomime looked positively radiant by comparison. I never knew if they were sisters or not but if they were not, they should have been. Everyone has the right to be ugly but these two abused that privilege. Somebody said one of them had been the model for a local artist who was painting a picture of the Medusa, but how true this was I never found out and Perseus certainly never appeared in my time as a library ticket holder.

Whenever I entered the hallowed inner sanctum of this concrete construction one of the ugly sisters shadowed me like a well-trained lap dog. They patently felt I was up to no good and that they were in grave danger of losing some of their prized chattels. Had I had the furtive, skulking deportment of Gormless Gregory then I could have understood their disquiet, but the only thing I wanted was to borrow a book or two.

This close attention turned into something of a game and I would deliberately turn back on myself whilst going down one of the beautifully polished lino passageways. At times this caused a collision and an embarrassed spluttering of apologies from my shadow who then pretended to straighten up the books on the nearest shelf to the location of the impact. Crouching behind a row of books was another little charade that amused my fertile brain, whilst the librarian peered in all directions wandering where I had vanished to. Why they did not do something useful totally bemused me but did not keep me from my jolly japes.

I occasionally made up the title of a book and invented a fictitious author then asked one of the ugly sisters if they had a copy of this bogus publication. Nowadays the computer would produce the answer in seconds but in those antediluvian days things were not so simple. I would take great delight watching them go through all the cards to see if such a volume was in their charge. I would have died of fright if they had produced a copy of what I had requested.

This cat and mouse game became tiresome so I decided to look farther afield for my literate gratification. Folton library was only a mile and a bit away and was housed in a far grander structure, being built of brick with double doors at the entrance and much more suited to my delicate sensitivity.

A change of address would be needed for me to enrol but I did not see this as a problem, as I had an auntie who lived on the same road and I could use hers for this purpose. After the necessary form filling and oath taking to do one's best for god, the queen and the country, dib, dib, dib, dob, dob, dob, or whatever the procedure was for gaining membership of such an illustrious establishment, I found myself the proud possessor of two library cards. Gormless Gregory might have had two sweet ration books but he did not have two library cards so I felt quits. But there again he did not need two library cards; in fact he did not need one because he could not read. Nevertheless, my feeling of superiority was brought down to earth with a jolt when I came face to face with the librarians.

Up to now I had dealt with a lovely young darling of a girl whom I thought I could at least dream about, but it turned out she was only helping out and actually worked in the council offices in some financial position. The actual librarians were the very same two old battleships from Upshaw. It seemed both libraries at that period were only part time and were easily managed by the same staff.

That really put the fly in the ointment. There was no way those two 'visions of loveliness' would not recognise me and have me arrested for false representation, treason, arson, blackmail, sedition or whatever mendaciously belonging to two different libraries came under on the statute books, and have me incarcerated in Strangeways Prison to await transportation to Van Diemen's Land.

I contemplated wearing a wig or one of our Daisy's dresses and a pair of glasses to fool them, but decided this was a bit drastic even for me, and what if I was recognised in a dress, I would have to jump ship to my Cousin Martha in Australia. Anyway, Mrs Blinkwell who lived next door to my Auntie Gertrude was a member of Folton and had known me since I was born. She would certainly blow the gaff. My dad would find out from someone in the Legion and my mum would then think about having to pay money to a brick library for books I had failed to return and life for me would become insufferable. I decided it was not worth the bother and never went again to Folton library.

***

November 5th, Guy Fawkes night, or bonfire night as we called it, was something special. It started sometime in August with us gathering anything that would burn and storing it until the special night arrived. Keeping it dry was the main object, well second main object really. The first was to stop it being nicked by a rival gang from another entry. Stealing of bonfire wood was an acceptable occupation. Not getting caught was the prime aim of the bonfire material 'nicker' and we knew we were on our own if apprehended in the art of plundering. Retribution was usually swift and painful but worth the risk. It became a matter of pride how much bonfire gear could be pilfered without the original owners realising who had done the snaffling. If you could keep the stolen material until November 5th, and burn it on your own bonfire, great pride would be felt and the original owners of the plunder would be told about it as soon as possible after the event. That is, told from a distance.

I remember being told that during world war two when the ack ack soldiers were on duty at the end of our entry, the gang dressed our Neil up as Guy Fawkes in old rags and put a mask over his face. They all agreed he looked better that way and put him in an old pram that would have been burned on the bonfire but for the blackout regulations. They wheeled him to the end of the entry and asked the soldiers for a 'penny for the guy'. The obliging artillerymen coughed up the asked for coinage but demanded to stick a banger in the guy's mouth and set it off. All agreed except

Neil who did not dare say anything for fear of reprisals from the group of soldiers for gaining pecuniary advantage. In went the banger and was duly lit by the glowing fag end of one of the British Armies finest troops. Bang went the fireworks. "*Bollocks*" shouted Neil and leapt out of the pram and dashed down the entry to the howls of laughter from the crowd behind him who thought the whole thing was hilarious.

As bonfire night approached the stack of rubbish to be burned would be piled up in the square situated half way along our entry. Our house was of the very large, Victorian, terraced type found in and around large cities, with a main road to the front and a cobbled entry running along the back. The back entry was the hub of the world for us kids, where the outside rarely penetrated. We felt safe and secure in the entry and were extremely territorial. We had back gardens as opposed to back yards which were found in some quarters of the town, but Monet's place in Giverny had nothing to worry about.

Working class people in those days were too busy trying to earn a living to have much time or spare cash to spend on their surroundings, so most gardens were just play areas of grass and soil. They were, however, jealously protected by high wooden fences painted with creosote once a year to preserve their longevity. The square in which our bonfire was built was surrounded by such fences that were in grave danger of igniting every November 5th.

Mrs Bradman, the town gossip, who thought for some reason best known to her, that I was a handsome little lad, (I'd heard her telling a neighbour) had a garden backing onto the square. She did not like bonfire night and thought it should be banned. She raised objections every year but was always overruled because everybody thought she was a busybody and should emigrate to Canada where her daughter had gone to live some years before. I did not think she should go because she was the only one who thought I was handsome, and anyway, I liked her Alsatian dog called Sally. One year her fence caught fire and the smell of burning tar and creosote was delightful. Mr. Nunn, Skiver's dad, worked speedily to put it out, being qualified to do so, as he was the chief auxiliary fireman at our local station. He did not fluster easily which was a good quality to have for a fire chief and quickly had the blaze under control, amid much booing and whistling from the rag bags who stood around him offering little or no help. Mrs Bradman was less than pleased and we were less than bothered.

How we were not all burned to death before November 5th remains an enigma, considering the dens we built inside the bonfires which would become our HQ until 'B' day arrived. Rival gangs would sneak up and set fire to the stack whilst we were still inside and we had to act like lightening to avoid a full-scale blaze. We, of course, reciprocated and tried to burn them to death, but no serious injuries were ever experienced by any of us in our back entries, more by luck than judgement I suspect.

Mrs Bradman blamed our Neil for the burning of her fence seeing he was older than me and had the responsibility for the location of the bonfire in the square and its erection. He was often unlucky in a number of ways by finding himself in the wrong place at the wrong time. On one particular occasion he should have been miles away because the incident was quite painful. My mother had a rather short fuse and when aroused became what might be classed as violent. She would throw anything that came to hand no matter what it was, and the eventual consequences of her outburst were never contemplated, at least by her. Sam, my brother who was older than Neil, had been back chatting her and was managing to wind her up to breaking point. This point was reached just as Neil entered the kitchen where the rumpus was taking place. Out shot mother's hand and clasped hold of a 2lb claw hammer resting from it's labours on the side of the sink and hurled it in the direction of Sam's head. The trajectory was intercepted by Neil's right shoulder which took the full impact of the would be assassination weapon and the words '*bollocks*' were heard once again to issue forth from his tortured, twisted mouth. Neil received no words of apology but a rather vexed reference was made to him standing in the way of retribution. Had the hammer found its intended target only the Lord knows what the consequences would have been.

***

The rag-and-bone man was a person who bought and sold discarded clothing, furniture, bric-a-brac, ornaments or anything, in fact, that was saleable. In exchange for articles he took, he often gave you a 'donkey stone'. This was a piece of pumice used to clean and whiten front door steps, and probably got its name 'donkey' because of the drudgery involved. Great pride was taken by the mothers along the row as to whose house had the cleanest step.

It was possible to barter with the rag man for anything

that took your fancy on his handcart (or horse pulled cart if he was posh). For those who do not remember the rag-and-bone man, television did a very good sit-com called 'Steptoe and Son' about the life of such men. You always knew when he was around for he would shout at the top of his voice alerting you that he was willing to relieve you of unwanted treasures. His cry of 'rag-bone' was usually unintelligible, sounding to us like 'sam-bone', and this is what we called him – the sam-bone man.

One time, our Neil did a bit of business with him. I do not know what Neil gave in exchange but he received a statue, made of white pottery, of a lady posed with one arm raised in the air and standing on one leg. It stood about two feet high and was quite grotesque. Neil slept on his own, unlike John and I who shared, in a single bed in the back attic. He, being older than us, was allowed to have a chest of drawers in his room on which he placed the statue. For reasons best known to him he called the white lady 'The Doon'. I think it was probably something to do with Lorna Doone, because he was a romantic teenager at the time, but he would never admit to this. Neil told me that on moon-lit nights, when the lunar radiance shone through his attic window, the Doon came to life and would dance around the room. He said he joined it in its macabre masque stating, "I dance with the Doon by the light of the moon." This, of course, scared the living daylights out of me. My imagination ran wild.

It was mother's practice on wash days to send me round the bedrooms to collect any dirty, discarded clothing laying on chairs, floors, beds or wherever, and bring it down to the scullery to be washed. This was OK until I reached the back attic, with the Doon sitting on the chest of drawers watching and daring me to enter. She always knew when I approached the door. I could feel her stare and sense her mocking smile. Clinging to the walls of that room, I would make my way gingerly round to the chair on the far side. Many a week Neil's shirts went un-washed because I had been too frightened to enter the Doon's domain. Neil would often have a go at mum for having missed his washing, but I always maintained that there had not been any when I looked in the attic. Whatever happened to that white lady is a mystery, but this I do know, if she is still around, I'll wager she is still up to her mischief when the moon is at its zenith.

***

In the early 1950's a Polish family moved into the house next door to Mrs Bradman, which did not exactly meet with her approval. I am not saying she was stuck up or xenophobic but I remember her saying to my mum one time that foreigners were alright but should stay in their own country.

This family had been interned in the same misplaced persons' camp as my mate Archie, but had been luckier than he by remaining together. The family consisted of mum and dad, a daughter of about sixteen called Danuta and a son a year or two younger than me. There was also a grandmother whom they referred to as 'Babushka', a lovely lady about two hundred and sixty years old, who still ruled the roost with a no nonsense approach. The young boy was called Rishu, which we assumed was Polish for Richard, so we called him Dick, much to the consternation of Babushka whose English was limited and did not know what we were talking about when we asked if Dick could come out to play. They had an unpronounceable surname so were referred to as 'The Polish Family'.

Dad Pole (we thought this was funny because it sounded like tadpole) had a way of keeping people at arm's length, not surprising considering what he and his family must have gone through during and just after the war. He must have had some handy connection though, because within a year of moving next to Mrs Bradman, he had opened a shop adjacent to the British Legion and was selling all kinds of strange looking meat and round sausage things to anyone adventurous enough to venture in. He called it by that name I had learned from Archie, 'The Delicatessen'. It was the first delicatessens I remember being opened in the whole of the Manchester area.

We never bought anything from his shop because my mother said you could never tell what these foreigners ate, it could be anything, and she did not want us all poisoned. Mrs Bradman said he should only be allowed to sell to his own kind and never went anywhere near the place. However, somebody must have bought his merchandise because within no time at all he had opened a second shop and moved his family to a more salubrious area of the city. Mrs Bradman said it was a bloody cheek the way foreigners came over here and took bread out of our mouths. I heard that her daughter was doing very nicely in Canada thank you very much.

***

Mrs Onions lived in the avenue that tagged onto the end of our entry. We did not give her a sobriquet because we considered her real name was funny enough. She was very snooty and I am sure she pronounced her name as O'Nions to her superior circle of friends, but we would have none of that and called her by her real name of Mrs ONIONS. Kids can be awfully cruel.

We took particular pleasure in shouting, "Good morning Mrs Onions; Good afternoon Mrs Onions," whenever we spotted her out shopping. Most of the neighbours we treated with indifference but we always made a point of calling a greeting to her. She had two Dachshunds, or sausage dogs to us, that waddled alongside her wherever she went and this, along with a 'nose in the air' carriage gave her the persona of a Walt Disney character. Sometimes we called out in devilment, "Sausages and onions," and then disappeared before we were spotted.

She had a little niece by the name of Barbara who frequently stayed at her house and went to one of our local Sunday Schools. She always wore pink and was spotlessly clean whatever the occasion. Her prissy prissy bearing got right up our noses and we would do our best to dirty her dress or blacken her knees by bumping into her and knocking her to the ground, accidentally of course. She looked as if she should be saying, "I'll skweam and skweam 'til I'm sick," but, in fact, said very little at all.

I am sure she thought we were rough and ready and somewhat unkempt and not to be consorted with, for we never had the pleasure of her company at our bonfire get together or any other gathering of the gang. She was far too grand for that and we were glad she was.

Barbara probably grow up to be a very beautiful woman because she was a pretty little thing, but was like a fish out of water in our area. I suspect that her none association with our lot could only be to her long term benefit but I bet she didn't have as much fun as we did.

***

I belonged to several Sunday Schools, not at the same time but at various periods of my childhood. It all depended on which one was giving the best offer. If the Baptists were going to Southport this year for a day trip, then I would be a member of the Baptist Sunday school. When the Congregationalists were having a grand Christmas party then my allegiance was to their way of worship and so it went on throughout the year. I think the most Sunday Schools I belonged to in one year was four. I am sure the teachers and elders of the church were wise to this scam but never turned anyone away from their doors, which was a good Christian thing to do and worthy of the message they were trying in vain to get across.

However, this oscillation of religious preference did come unstuck on occasions, especially around Whitsuntide, that festival celebrating the descent of the Holy Spirit to the apostles. If caught as a member of a Sunday School at this time of year then my spirit descended as well, as I would be required to take part in those sickly, sissy, best behaviour processions, the 'Whit Walks' that wound around the town. All the Sunday Schools in the area took part and paraded their banners with great pride. One was required to adorn a spotless white shirt, a pair of pumps, freshly whitened with blanco, grey short pants (that's if you were a boy, the girls had their own mode of dress), and a clean face. The most upsetting part of the whole show was the fact that one had to stand where one was put in the line up and this could lead to being placed next to Mrs Onions' niece Barbara.

The whole town turned out to watch the procession wind its way around the main roads of the area, with Mrs Onions saying how charming little Barbara looked and Mrs Bradman saying how lovely Freddie looked today, especially walking next to Barbara who was resplendent in her pink dress. This was more than my ego could stand. I often feigned sickness on Whit Sunday to escape the dreaded parade, claiming to have contacted beri beri, St. Vitis dance or elephantiasis, but my mother was wise to these antics and would have none of it. If I could go on the trips to the seaside, she said, and enjoy the Christmas parties then I could jolly well show my appreciation by taking part in their pageant. To me this meant making a spectacle of myself and my macho demeanour suffered a shattering blow.

***

9

Sports lessons at school were my favourite activities but I also enjoyed history, and one particular lesson had such an affect on me I re-lived the event in my out-of-school life. We had been given a lesson about the Kon-Tiki Expedition of 1947, where Thor Heyerdahl, a Norwegian ethnologist, along with five others, built a raft out of balsa wood and sailed it from Peru to the Pacific Islands. This was done to prove it was possible for some tribe or other to have migrated from South America to Polynesia. We were shown pictures of the raft and watched an 8mm cine film (no video in those days) of the event. I was not bothered about the ethnological aspect or the fact that the original Kon Tiki had been a sun king who had migrated with the white settlers into the Pacific.

No, to me Kon Tiki was a beautiful boat. It made such an impression that Skiver, Don and I decided we would build our own Kon-Tiki and see if we could have more luck with it than we had with our canoe. Balsa wood was out of the question so orange boxes would have to substitute. Visiting my favourite librarians at the Golden Hill Park library produced a book containing a picture of Kon-Tiki, so we were up and running. We had our blue print.

Old fruit boxes were collected from all the greengrocers in the area and kept in my cellar. I had to guard them like the crown jewels otherwise they would have finished up on the back of the fire one of the family had to light every morning in the big old cast iron range. This range had to be black leaded every Saturday morning with Zebo Grate Polish. What a job! I volunteered to make the fire for the foreseeable future, which was accepted with a certain amount of suspicion, but it was safer this way. We had huge cellars in our house and plenty of tools were always lying around, especially 2lb claw hammers, so it was good sense to build our ocean going craft there.

Much debate went on as to the best way of achieving our objective and occasionally Gormless Gregory turned up uttering useless gibberish for us to consider. We usually sent him away to nick biscuits or something so as we could get on with the more serious problems of construction. Nails, string and some awful smelling glue, which had to be boiled in an old pan Skiver's mother provided, were gathered together and the job was underway.

After a couple of weeks of painstaking labour we discovered our lovingly constructed masterpiece would not go out through the cellar door no matter which way we turned it. Don blamed it on Skiver who blamed it on me because it was my cellar. I blamed it on both of them, maintaining they were both cleverer than I and should not have let me have my way in the situation of the shipyard. Gormless Gregory said he had been trying to tell us this all along but kept getting sent away to nick biscuits. After much thinking and talking we decided it would have to be 'unbuilt' and taken out bit by bit for re-construction in the garden, even if it meant getting rained on. After all the ultimate object was to get the raft wet anyway.

Amongst much mumbling, grumbling and rumbling the tour de force was taken to pieces and carefully re-located in the back garden. Much of it was broken beyond repair and had to be remade from scratch, which did not please us one little bit. Many of the nails were bent and could not be hammered straight again so new ones had to be found from somewhere. We had purloined the original ones from our respective dad's collection of bits and pieces, but to do the same again was chancing our luck a wee bit too far. How could I explain to my dad that his carefully collected ironmongery was destined for Polynesia and not the back fence that was in need of urgent attention! Skiver and Don had similar problems so we had to find a new supplier. Gormless Gregory. If he could take just a handful at a time from the chandlers on Bank Road we could have the job done in no time at all. But stealing was not the way to get to the Pacific Islands. As much as Gregory pleaded with us to let him nick the goods we would not agree to larceny, so if he could not steal them honestly we would do without.

But we could not do without. No nails, no raft. The problem seemed insurmountable. We tried various ways of holding the craft together but nothing seemed to work. We had exhausted our string supply and glue will only take so much weight before it gives up the ghost. Two or three days after admitting to being abject failures and being somewhat depressed, Skiver came knocking on my door, tunelessly whistling as was his wont. Skiver was always whistling. In fact his incessant warbling drove us potty. But this day was different and I could have forgiven him almost anything, for in his hand was a brown paper bag full of shiny nails. He said he had gone to see Mr Lampton, the chandler, and told him about our predicament. Mr. Lampton had done no more than fill a bag full of nails and given them to Skiver for nothing. I had never thought of being honest and just asking for them but was over the moon to think the South Seas was once again in our sights. Gormless Gregory said it was plain stupid, he could have nicked them just as easily.

We completed the re-ship in next to no time and decided another grand launch would be in order. The Mersey beckoned and we obliged with another parade to the meadows with the admiring public gazing on in amazement at our achievement. God, how superior we felt as an entourage of the nations youth gathered behind us and escorted us to the slipway. Don won the toss of who should be first on the raft and Skiver and I raised no objections. Into the water it went to the accompaniment of cheers and a few jeers. "Oh ye of little faith," I hollered at the crowd as Don stepped onto Kon Tiki. Don fell off Kon Tiki. Straight into the 'oggin' went he amid much clapping and laughter. Kon Tiki shot off down stream to be lost for ever in the swirling rapids of the Mersey. We decided there and then that shipbuilding was not for us. Later in life Don would fall off a much larger sea going craft.

***

When not engaged in building vessels for the ocean, we tried our hand at constructing land bound vehicles or soapboxes as we knew them. These were our version of formula one and if assembled correctly would be the envy of all other gangs in the locality. Whenever a set of wheels became available, either thrown out because they were buckled or had outlived their usefulness as part of babies prams, etc. we would pounce. We built the chassis out of any old wood laying around and attached the wheels and axle to make a cart, or soapbox. A seat of sorts would be fashioned and string or rope attached to the front axle acted as the steering mechanism.

Two sets of wheels were normally required but not always necessary as three wheeler soapboxes were often just as good as four wheelers. We raced these contraptions up and down the cobbled entry and what a bone shaking experience it was. The wheels and axles would buckle and bend at regular intervals due to the rough terrain they encountered, but these minor problems were soon put right by our expert usage of a four pound sledge hammer. The carts were propelled by 'boy power' and it was quite a hairy experience for the driver if his pusher was a good sprinter and a show off. Sometimes the pusher used a stick as the means of propulsion by placing it on the back of the soapbox and pushing. Often the stick slipped forward and entered the back of the driver who would curse unholy words aimed at the pusher, accusing him of doing it on purpose. I personally received many a cut rear end by this method. On one occasion, John O'Sullivan blamed my younger brother Rodney of 'stabbing' him on purpose, jumped off the soapbox and bloodied our Rodney's nose. I am not convinced that John was wrong.

The most frightening times were when we were pushed

downhill, usually from Upshaw Bridge down Station Road and on to the station approach. The speeds achieved would put the willies up the most hardened driver, and many a grazed arm and leg were the result of too much bravado from the boy power. The scariest thing about this downhill run was the railings at the bottom which stopped one from going onto the station platform. Many a soapbox finished up wrapped around these railings with the driver nursing his cuts and bruises and mumbling such things as, "*It didn't hurt, it didn't hurt.*"

We held long distance races, or marathons as we called them, down Folton Road, along Beech Avenue, back down Moorland Road, onto Bank Road and down our entry, a distance of about three miles. Often, after waiting what seemed like hours, the spectators were treated to the sight of the driver and his pusher carrying bits and pieces of their broken soapbox as they entered the entry. This was always the signal for great mirth and levity to take place amongst the watchers and no feeling of sympathy or concern was ever shown no matter how serious the participants thought the matter was.

***

Rob Reynold moved into the house next door to Skiver, well into the upstairs flat really, because the house had been divided into two parts. The downstairs was taken over by the Women's Voluntary Service, or W.V.S. (it had not yet received its royal charter) who were doing sterling work looking after those less fortunate than the rest of us. I had thought of going to see if they had any green goalkeeper's jumpers, but when I saw the myriad of wheelchairs lining the hallway and filling the lean to at the rear entrance, I decided they probably had more important things on their minds than ungreen goalies.

Rob arrived with his mother from somewhere in the Folton area and was of like age to myself. He was somewhat of a loner, which was not surprising considering the life he led at home. His father was unknown to him but he had lots of 'uncles' who would turn up out of the blue and stay for an hour or two. Rob then had to vacate the quarters until uncle had gone and as this was 'the norm' it did not seem to worry him. Sometimes the uncle would stay all night and the lad would be required to keep a low profile by going to the pictures or hanging about on the park, often until it was too dark to see. On his return home, he went straight to his bedroom in the attic and would stay there until morning. By the time he had arisen from his slumbers, uncle had usually vacated but often a few shillings would be left for him in appreciation of his non-appearance. This arrangement was satisfactory to all parties and Rob was never short of a bob or two.

His mother was beautiful, in her early thirties and could have passed as a double for Simone Signore, the French film star. I used to fantasise about both of them, that is Rob's mother and Simone Signore, not Rob and his mother, and dream of going away with her in her Lee Francis car. I had never seen or heard of Lee Francis cars until Mrs. Reynold arrived with hers. It was a beauty and Rob said it was a gift from one of his uncles. At times she would let us sit in it and the smell of the leather upholstery was most gratifying. It was far too grand for the likes of me but I could dream couldn't I? Occasionally she would take us for a ride to Folton where she had some business or other. I never found out what that business was and I was not bothered. We would sit in the back and thought we were the bee's knees. Well I did, Rob was used to it and took it all in his stride.

I was the only one who seemed to play with Rob and I think this made me a little special in his mother's eyes. I am sure most kids had been told to stay away from him because of the way his mother earned her living. I was told no such thing because, for all her faults, my mother was not a bigot and most of the time she didn't know where I was anyway. Rob's mum promised on more than one occasion to take us both away on holiday sometime, but sadly this never happened. Being a busy lady, I assumed she had more important things to do. I never knew where she originally hailed from. She could have been highborn as she spoke well and presented a classy persona quite unlike the working class families I lived amongst. The incongruity of the W.V.S. downstairs and Mrs Reynold plying her trade upstairs was totally lost on me in my innocence.

Rob was a strange boy in many ways but had a number of endearing qualities. One of them was generosity. He had many playthings he shared with me without hesitation and countless pleasant hours were passed in his flat playing games and looking through his collection of books. His library was not as big as the one I had joined on Golden Hill Park but it was less intimidating. He always had a copy of the latest Dandy and Beano, those two prized comics that were my favourite read at that time, the Eagle comic still being a bit too erudite for me. His book collection contained publications such as Kidnapped, Treasure Island and Robinson Crusoe and many a wet day was idled away in another world far away from Upshaw's back entries.

One Christmas Rob received a proper leather football or 'casey' as we used to call them and he came around for me to go with him onto Golden Hill Park for a kick around. During our game my brother John appeared, swiped the ball from us and started to tease Rob by saying he would have to beg for it back. He was bigger and stronger than we were but no way was Rob going to beg for anything, so our John kicked the ball into the swings and roundabouts area which was surrounded by a ten foot high wire fence. The gates were locked on Sundays and bank holidays so the ball was beyond our reach until the gates were unlocked or a way could be found to scale the fence.

Remembering Skiver's dad was not only the local fire chief, but was also the council office caretaker and had keys to fit every lock in the whole world, we made our way to his house. He was a nice bloke and although it was Christmas morning he agreed to come and open the gate for us.

We arrived back at the park some ten minutes after leaving it to find the ball had disappeared and was never seen again. I do not know what ever happened to that ball or what explanation was given to his mother, but I do know our John never got the blame for its loss, and full credit goes to Rob for that.

Rob Reynold was sent away to an agricultural boarding school in Shropshire about eighteen months after moving into our area and his mother transferred herself somewhere on the south coast. I never saw either of them again but often think of Rob and his unusual lifestyle. I liked him.

***

Manchester City F.C. were as dodgy in those days as they are today and you never quite knew which team was going to turn out. It could be the one that would play the opposition off the park, or it might well be the one that would take a hammering and drive us all demented. It was the same set of players, more or less, that turned out each week but the transformation of form and desire to win had to be seen to be believed. 'City Slickers' would be the headlines in the Evening Chronicle's Football Pink one Saturday night whilst the next week one would be faced with 'City's Shame', glaring out at you like a biblical admonition. Consistency is a word that has never been a part of M.C.F.C.'s vocabulary.

Players like the legendary ex- German paratrooper turned goalkeeper Bert Trautman thrilled and delighted us week after week, except when he let in a handful of goals, which usually turned out not to be his fault anyway. He was signed from St. Helens Town and sadly had to overcome racial prejudice inflicted by a handful of bigots, it being so soon after the second world war, and did so magnificently. He made 545 appearances between 1949 and 1964 for the sky blues, the most famous being the 1956 F.A. Cup Final against Birmingham where he broke his neck. No substitutes were available in those days so Bert was forced to continue in goal for the last fifteen minutes of the game, unaware of the seriousness of his injury. From that moment on, if not before, Bert Trautman became a hero and his name was forever etched on the hearts of every Maine Road regular, and many who were not.

Roy Paul, the Welsh wizard and captain, and Ken Barns, who could dribble around the opposition until they were dizzy, gave us roll models we could look up to. There was big Dave Ewing a centre half whose motto seemed to be, 'If you go passed me I'll break both your legs.' He made today's so called hard men like Vinny Jones and Robbie Savage look like sissies. Little Bobby Johnstone, a Scottish international inside right who, it was alleged, trained on Guinness and needed a pint or two before stepping out to play on a Saturday afternoon. He had a beer belly any tap room regular would be proud of, yet he was brilliant and scored some of the most wonderful goals I have ever had the pleasure of witnessing. After he retired from football, Johnstone went into the food business, manufacturing pies that he supplied to Maine Road until well into the 1980s.

I had become a Manchester City supporter through Skiver's dad who had acquired a Riley motorcar sometime in the early fifties and took it out once a week for a trip to City's ground at Maine Road. Skiver, Don and myself went along for the ride and were bitten by the sky blue bug and enchanted by the blue moon. Before this, I had been a regular at Old Trafford shouting on the red half of Manchester, which just goes to show how fickle I was. Being a member of the school football team enabled me get free tickets from Manchester United for their home games, which was a good way for them to build up their support level. The very idea nowadays is unthinkable. How times have changed.

The ride in the Riley motorcar eventually won me over. It was as impossible in those days as it is today to support two teams from the same city, and anyway, both Skiver and Don had taken the oath to hate and despise Manchester United until their dying day, and they were my pals. Although I still drew my free ticket for Manchester United, I didn't use it myself but sold it (a juvenile ticket tout) for a thrupenny bit to Gormless Gregory who doubtless sold it on at a loss. I know he didn't go to the game himself as he had no interest in football whatsoever, and anyway, he could never have found Old Trafford on his own. I believe there was one occasion when he went unaccompanied to Stretford on a bus, but could not remember the bus number for the return journey and finished up in Altrincham. The local police called on his mother and requested she go and collect him as he was beginning to frighten the local populace.

It was the days before road parking restrictions and the dreaded traffic warden, so on match days one parked on any side street in the vicinity of the football ground. The earlier one arrived the nearer the stadium one got, but no matter where one finished up, it did not stop the local kids from descending on each car owner with a promise to 'Mind your car mister.' The fee for this was negotiable, but usually amounted to a few pennies. Once the account was settled, off would shoot the vagabonds to find the next sucker.

No 'car minding' was ever done of course, for the kids were never seen again until the next game when they would re-appear and the procedure would be re-enacted. The fear of what the wretches might do to your car if the tariff were not handed over usually meant that you paid up. One had to admire the entrepreneurial skills of these Moss Side mafioso, with their pockets bulging with lovely pennies.

***

10

One time when our Sam arrived home on leave from the RAF, he brought with him a border collie with the unlikely name of Laddie. Laddie had been kicked out of a farm for being idle whilst on sheep patrol, and Sam decided he would find a good home with us, even though mum and dad did not want a dog. We had an Alsatian at one time called Zenda, and a beautiful dog it was, but we were not really animal people and did not know how to look after such things properly. Zenda was given to a lady in Chorlton-cum-Hardy who loved dogs and had plenty of room for them to enjoy the freedom they deserve, and it was decided we would have no more pets. One look at Laddie changed all that. He was such a loveable thing he melted even the hardest heart, and no way could mum and dad agree to the alternative option of having him put down.

Laddie would curl up in front of the fire and go to sleep for hours on end, snoring his head off. He was just like a big hearth rug and stood for any amount of cuddling and fussing. Occasionally, when he could be bothered to get up, he would saunter into the entry to see what was going on with us noisy kids and sometimes join in the fun. But mostly, life was just a big yawn for him and he preferred the warmth and security of the kitchen. It was quite a job to get Laddie to go for a walk, although sometimes we did actually manage to drag him onto Golden Hill Park, but far from chasing balls or biting kids rear ends he elected to lie and watch the world go by. He was by far the laziest dog I have ever encountered and I suppose in retrospect there must have been something wrong with him, because by nature collies are workers and like to be on the go. The fact that we didn't think there was any cause for concern shows how ignorant and unfit we were to own a dog, and the thought we were not the only ones does not make it any better.

One day in the summer break from school, my mum called me from playing for what I thought would be another trip to the shops or the bookies, but this time it was different. Laddie was not at all well and needed to be taken to the People's Dispensary for Sick Animals, who parked their travelling hospital pantechnicon van on Turner's Timber Yard car park opposite the Essoldo cinema. Laddie was by then a huge dog who, at the best of times, found it difficult to walk, but now could not even stand. I summoned my mate John O'Sullivan to give me a lift to get Laddie into a wheelchair I had borrowed from the back entrance of the WVS. I was sure they would not mind me making use of their property for such a good cause and I would replace it when the PDSA man had made Laddie better.

It took some lifting for John and I to get this overweight canine into the chair which had a stamp saying 'W.V.S.

Property' on the side. The pair of us puffed and grunted with our burden up and over Upshaw Bridge, no mean feat I can tell you, and down Lower Road to the car park. We attracted some funny looks as we pushed the poor dog who was half covered in a blanket somebody produced from somewhere, but we cared not, our only concern was Laddie.

I gave the vet the shilling I had been given to put in the box for sick animals and helped him to carry Laddie up the steps into the back of the van. John and I waited outside whilst the vet carried out his examination, and it was not a pleasant wait. A short while later the vet came out and said there was nothing he could do as Laddie had distemper and would have to be put to sleep. I was heart broken but somehow managed to return the empty wheelchair to the rear entrance of the W.V.S. even though my vision was so blurred with tears and my throat ached. I returned later and pinned a note on the wheelchair saying, 'Thank You'. I do not suppose they ever found out what the note was for.

***

Apart from being a bookie's runner, one of the other foremost reasons for my presence on this earth was to look after my younger sisters, or so my mother thought and that was reason enough. By the time they were born she had clearly had enough of child minding. In fact, she had finished looking after kids before I was born. My sister Lana, who is fifteen years my senior, had brought me up and for a long time I thought she was my mother. Had Lana not bathed me or changed my clothing I would have stayed dirty and bedecked in muck-ridden garb.

Why did people go on having babies when they quite obviously did not want them or need them! This was one of the mysteries of the universe to me as a child and I am still not quite sure why people let it happen. It became my responsibility to keep my two little sisters amused. I was barely old enough to look after myself let alone two little girls, but that fact was not considered important by my mother who was one of the best delegators in the business. I was the only 'rider of the range' down our entry who had two little squaws to drag along with him. The only thing I could do was to put them in their pushchairs and pretend they were the chuck wagon.

One hot summer day I was out playing with Don and Skiver when the inevitable call came for me to report post-haste to our kitchen door. Caroline, the baby of the family, needed to be looked after, (Thelma, the next to the youngest, had obviously been farmed out elsewhere) and I was once again the lucky prize winner. God, what a drag, just as we three were about to head off to Barton Bridge which was quite some distance away. Barton Bridge spanned the Manchester Ship Canal and was a great attraction to us because it turned to let big ships pass on their way to all corners of the earth. The Bridgwater Aqueduct also crossed the Ship Canal at this point and was great fun to play around. There was only one thing to do and that was to put Caroline into her pushchair and bring her along. Mother would not mind, she never minded because, as I have said, she rarely knew where I was anyway.

Off we sped in great haste, Caroline in the chair getting bounced around all over the place. She could well put up with the rough ride, as she must have been at least twelve months old at the time, in fact almost old enough to look after herself. She was a lovely little kid who was no bother at all and was quite content to sit in her pushchair, which was just as well considering what happened to her that day. We arrived at Barton Bridge around noontime and went to work at our boat and barge spotting. I parked Caroline alongside the towpath on the Bridgwater Canal and told her to go to sleep as I had important business to attend to. Don, Skiver and I were up and down the towpath like rampaging Indians on the warpath completely forgetting about Caroline reposing in her stately carriage. After an hour or so we found ourselves, quite by accident, in the Manchester Oil Refinery unloading area and thought we had better skidaddle rather rapidly. The quickest way was over the railings and onto the main road that would head us in the direction of Albert Park and home.

We ran like the wind for the whole three miles or so back to our entry before Mr. Manchester Oil Refinery found out we had been trespassing in his works. Caught in such a place, could have resulted in us being locked up forever and the key being thrown away. We had been lucky to escape so rewarded ourselves with a game of football on Golden Hill Park. One of us suggested we go for a swim in the Mersey but realising it was probably too late in the day, decided to leave it for another time.

It was around four in the afternoon when I returned to our kitchen to get a drink of water.

" Where's the baby?" asked mother. " What baby?" I replied. Crikey, I had left Caroline sleeping in her pushchair some four hours earlier at Barton Bridge. Mother nearly had a fit and started to rant and rave. I thought the best thing for me to do was to beat a hasty retreat and retrace my steps back to Barton to find out if by any chance our Caroline was still there. She could not have moved herself as she was too little, but the gypsies could have pinched her, as I knew they did that sort of thing. I broke the four-minute mile barrier long before Roger Banister but it was never recorded. When I arrived back at Barton Bridge there was Caroline fast asleep in her pushchair like a good little girl, none the worse for her experience. Mild sunstroke perhaps but nothing worse. Like dad when mum and Daisy almost drowned, I could not make out what all the fuss was about. It's just as well that we did not go for the suggested swim though.

***

Shilton, the local greengrocer whose back door opened onto our entry, threw the empty fruit and vegetable boxes out of the back door to await collection and onward transportation to the tip. A red Bedford truck was used for this task and was driven by a huge man by the name of Henry who worked part time for them removing the rubbish. His full time employer was British Railways, as it was known at that time, where he inspected the track to make sure it was fit for trains to run on. I often gave Henry a lift to load up the Bedford and would go with him to the tip at the side of Upshaw meadows to dispose of the garbage. I loved the ride in the lorry but the main attraction was the tip itself. The smell of all that refuse was delightful and I hoped when I grew up I would be able to get a job as a tip man. My ambitions were boundless.

Henry quite often had an easy day because Shilton were the main supplier of our shipbuilding material as well as a provider of our kindling. It was a race between all the kids of the area to see who could get there first, and woe betide me if the O'Sullivans or the Jacksons beat me to it. The noise of the boxes being thrown onto the cobbles was the signal for all other activity to be brought to a temporary halt whilst the dash for the smelly timber took place. It was an unwritten law that any football, cricket, tickey, hopscotch, or any other Olympian pursuit could be halted and restarted at the same point after the collection of the firewood. All the kids strictly adhered to the rules and there was never any falling out over who collected the discarded boxes. It was the one who got to Shilton's back door first that had the right to the spoils, and often we would help each other to carry the booty to our respective homes, even when we had lost the race. This sometimes hurt, especially when shipbuilding was in progress, but we never cheated on this unwritten code and the slipway had to wait if we lost the race.

Shilton's was run by Stuart one of the sons of the shop's founder, he being 'Old Mr.Shilton', a man as ancient as Methuselah but twice as scary. He looked like Maurice Chevalier, always wore a straw boater with a red band and a red carnation in his buttonhole. His face had been reddened by too much whiskey. He would sit on a chair on the pavement outside his shop and watch the world go by, especially the pretty young women, though how he could see them was something of a puzzle, he being always 'three sheets to the wind'. He got that way by spending a great deal of time at the bar of the Conservative Club five doors up the road. I was frightened of him because he had a habit of staring at you without saying a word, and his gaze would follow you up the street. He was probable thinking, "There goes that thieving little tow-rag who pinches all my boxes."

Next door to Shilton's was 'The Dairy' run by Maurice Chevalier's daughter Jane who was one of the loveliest people you could ever meet. She could not have been more different from her brother Stuart who was a real 'flash Harry' and would rob you blind, even though you had very little to start with. Jane would rather give you something than sell it to you and how she stayed in business for so long is a mystery. She had a white Alsatian dog called Duke, one of the most vicious brutes ever to draw breath. It was not allowed out on its own because it would have eaten people, or that is what we thought, but occasionally it escaped from the flat above the shop and would terrorise the area. When Duke appeared un-chaperoned the streets would clear and the air raid siren would sound a warning to people of the impending doom. It was rumoured that Duke had been cashiered out of the German Army on account of her savage nature, but we did not really buy that one.

Jane was married to Graham an ex RAF officer who looked every inch the part. He had a huge, ginger, handlebar moustache and drove an open top M.G. sports car that had all the heads turning whenever he went passed, as cars of such splendour were a rare sight in our neck of the woods. Graham was Terry Thomas with a bit of Jimmy Edwards thrown in if such an entity can be visualised, and kept himself very much in the background when it came to the activities of the shop. He and Jane made an incongruous pair, she being homely and human and he being somewhat brash and cartoonish. We never shopped at Jane's because my mum said she had bought some cheese from her at one time and it had gone mouldy within a day. I think it was more likely to be the fact that Jane did not have a tick book!

***

11

The Co-op was the place for tick books and they paid you for shopping with them by way of dividend or 'divi' as it was known. To me it seemed magic that by sticking a check onto a piece of sticky sheet, a bit like the fly paper that hung near the centre light in our kitchen, you could get money from the manager. You got about four shillings back for every pound spent. The intricacies of the system were unknown to me as a child but, suffice to say, that every divi day I was given a monetary treat and that is all I needed to know. I had earned it, being the one who had to spend precious playtime waiting in the queue at the Co-op counter to be served with half a pound of cheese or a dozen eggs, which would be put on the tick book. Pay at the end of the week.

I got sick of reading the notice pinned to the wall that said, 'Join the Co-op, it's the divy that counts'. It did not count very loud otherwise I would have heard it and I heard nothing but the whirr of the hand operated bacon slice. I used to ogle wide eyed at the large, open, square tins of biscuits on display in front of the counter, and think to myself how nice it would be if one could help oneself to a bagful of Crawfords Maryland. My muscles should have been Herculean the amount of times I trudged home with twenty pounds of spuds and two or three cabbages for the weekend dinner, and struggling home with a dozen loaves was not an unusual occurrence.

I could well have done with one of those bikes used by the Co-op boys to deliver the orders. They had a big carrying frame on the front which held boxes of groceries and had a metal plate advertising CWS Carbolic Soap or CWS Health Salts or some other CWS product.

We always got our weekend joint of meat free of charge from Terry's Butchers in Folton, another hike for me every Friday evening. Before I was born our family had lived in Folton on the same road as the second library I joined, and on occasions mum and dad went out for the evening to the Bird in Hand pub on Folton Road, passing Terry's Butchers on the way. One night on the return journey dad noticed the inside of the butcher's shop was ablaze and sent mum to telephone for the fire brigade. Being quite a handy sort of bloke he smashed his way into the shop and set about extinguishing the flames.

The shop was part of a terraced row of dwelling houses and the situation could have become catastrophic but for his heroic and prompt action. By the time the fire brigade arrived the situation was under control and the shop had not suffered as badly as it might have done. Mr. Terry's gratitude was such that he promised mum and dad a free weekend joint of meat for life. This offer was thankfully accepted and utilized until the butcher died many years later. Mother never forgave him for dying saying it was most inconsiderate of him and our meat ration would have to be curtailed somewhat as a result.

There were occasions when ready cash was available and the Co-op tick book would not be required. I would be sent to Shilton's for the twenty pounds of spuds and a couple of large onions or cabbages. This was one of the chores I hated most because I knew the last chapter off by heart. The routine was, on my return home the burden would be lightened by two of the largest potatoes in the bag. I would then be sent back to the shop to complain that I had been short changed as mum had weighed the spuds and they had not come to twenty pounds. I was never good at this sort of thing and I am sure it must have shown on my face, but invariably I would get the difference just to avoid a scene.

However, sometimes Stuart would argue the toss and I would go home empty handed. This was the cue for mum to go storming off to the shop and accuse the plutocrats of ripping off the working man who grafted hard enough for his crust without the likes of Stuart Shilton taking the bread out of her babies' mouths. This inevitably did the trick because for all his wealth Stuart was frightened of my mother, and bad customer relations was something he could do without.

Maurice Chevalier sat on his chair outside the doorway, grinning like a Cheshire cat, with his straw boater at a rakish angle, thinking the whole show was hilarious and worth the entrance money. Nothing like this ever took place at the bar of the Conservative Club. The theatricals mum played out have left their scar on my psyche even to this day, where I cannot return goods to shops, even though they are faulty, without feeling a pang of guilt.

***

Meals in our house were always silent (very puritanical). Dad would have no talking whatsoever at the table as he considered it bad manners and ungodly to converse whilst eating. If we violated his rules he would let us know in no uncertain way, by either pointing his knife or his fork in our faces stating he would teach us manners if it was the last thing he did. The thought of losing an eye or having four puncture holes in our nose usually taught us manners and silence prevailed for the rest of the meal.

We had a roast dinner every Saturday always drowned in mum's own very special gravy. She made this gravy brown by burning a spoon and adding sugar, but how this worked I never found out. It tasted absolutely awful but no matter how much pleading I did for her not to put any on my plate, it made no difference. "Oh shurrup," she would say, and drench my plate with that dreaded sauce. It spoiled many an otherwise good dinner. We had tinned fruit and Carnation milk for afters, or one of mum's home made rice puddings with a thick skin of leathery milk on top. Sometimes she would make bread pudding from any stale bread there was laying around and this would linger in my stomach like a lump of lead. I hated it, nevertheless had no alternative but to eat what was put in front of me. To this day, the very mention of bread pudding churns my insides into spasms of revulsion.

Any leftover meat would be eaten on a Sunday when another roast dinner would be served up, to be eaten once again in complete silence. Weekend dinners were compulsory, where all the family were required to attend. One had to have a very good reason for not being there, like being dead! During the week, dinners were more relaxed and informal affairs where strict attendance was not always required. Mind you, if mum had made a meal and you failed to attend, words would be spoken and the prepared repast would have to be eaten cold or warmed up if you were lucky. More often than not weekday meals were meat free, a bowl of Oxo with bread, or mushrooms in milk, being the standard fare.

On occasions, sausage was on the menu but usually restricted to one each. One of these sausage meals stays in my mind because for me it turned out to be 'sausage free'. We sat down to a plate of mashed potato and sausage, one each, and my brother John was sitting next to me on the long bench that ran the length of the oil clothed kitchen table. He pointed to something in the far corner of the kitchen ,where all our meals were taken, and nodded for me to follow his stare. This, of course, I did but could see nothing.

I looked back to see my plate of mashed potato was sausageless. John's cheeks were bulging and a self satisfied grin creased his face. I did not dare speak out loud for fear of a perforated nose or loss of an eye and all I could manage was a kick of his shins under the table, whilst being told to behave myself by my mother. I thought this was grossly unfair. Not only was I sausageless, but I got the blame as well. It went through my mind that if our John committed murder, I would probably be culpable and hanged by the neck until I was dead. Oh well, I didn't like sausages very much anyway.

***

The milkman also suffered as a result of my mum's shadow boxing with the truth. In fact, all tradesmen were fair game when it came to the art of prevarication but 'Ernie' came off worst. One of her favourites was to send me out to ask the 'milkie' for an extra pint as our Sammy was coming home on leave from the RAF. When the milkman, who was named Ernie incidentally, knocked for his money on Saturday morning, I hid in the cellar because I knew beyond doubt mum would state quite categorically she had had no any extra milk that week, and whoever said she had was a liar.

There were very few people around brave enough to call

my mum a liar and Ernie was no exception. "But Freddie asked for an extra pint because Sammy was coming home on leave," Ernie pleaded. "Where's our Freddie, the buggeroo, I'll kill him when I get my hands on him; our Sammy is not due home for another two weeks," mum would holler as though she had been cursed with kids that did not know honesty if it hit them between the eyes. 'Buggeroo' was one of her favourite words. Whether this was a bastardisation of 'buckaroo', as in cowboy, or not I do not know. 'Pig's melt' was another name we were called on a regular basis, and it was not meant as a compliment, but I could not even guess where this one came from.

The denial of extra milk was all a facade, of course, but played out with such reality it almost convinced me I had purloined the milk on my own initiative. I can not see how Ernie did not know the truth but he usually conceded he must have made a mistake, either to save me from a hiding or because it made life easier, and perhaps it was the Jones's up the street who had had the extra. There were many variations on this theme but they usually ended with the same result, mum getting something gratis and feeling she was quite entitled to it. Ernie was a genial character who never seemed to have an off day and was loved by all the old ladies for his kindness and helpfulness. He would do all sorts of favours for his customers like dropping in order books to the Co-op and delivering messages between old folk who could no longer get about as well as they used to do. I eventually went to work for him on his milk float for a period of about two years.

It happened like this. Around seven o'clock every morning I had to collect the Daily Dispatch or whatever morning newspaper was in vogue in our house at the time, from Clelland's, the local newsagent. The paper mum took depended on which racing tipster was having the best run of luck and had nothing to do with the political stance of the publication or anything else. In fact, on voting day mother would call up the local Labour party and ask if they could provide a car to take her to the polling station. They always did and she always voted Conservative. I never found out why she did not call for a Conservative car but perhaps it was to prevent the neighbours knowing how she voted, because the cars always advertised their party, and of course Labour was the working man's lot.

On my way back from Clelland's I ran into Ernie who was dashing around like a whirling dervish because he had slept in that morning and was late. He asked if I could give him a lift and he would drop me at school before nine o'clock which was the assembly time. I asked my mum if this was O.K. but she wanted to know how much he would pay me. By the time I found Ernie again to ask him how much he was three streets away. He said, "Seven and six a week." I was delighted and dashed home to tell my mum, "Seven and six a week." " Tell him ten bob and he's got a helper," she said. I galloped off to find that Ernie was another couple of streets further away and told him what mum had said. "Right." he agreed. I was then too whacked to be of much help that day having covered half the streets in the area at break neck speed, without having breakfasted. However, I was to be of great help to him over the next couple of years and the extra cash came in handy at home.

***

12

It was about this time that Mr Spalding, the man who stood on Upshaw Station approach and sold the evening papers out of a bag, was looking for someone to do a delivery round for him. My mum volunteered me for this chore, stating I had nothing to do after school and it would only take me about an hour. I could not thank her enough as this would extend my working day from seven in the morning until about six in the evening. What more could I ask for! Much joy, I do not think. I was under age, the minimum being thirteen and I was only twelve, had no bike and needed to pass a medical given by the local authority, I told them. I was told in return that none of this mattered as nobody gave a hoot for the regulations and our John had an old bike I could use. That was it, all settled, done and dusted.

The morning milk round was great because Ernie was good fun and I got to ride on the electric milk float. I could also help myself to the orange juice we carried in those half pint bottles before I went to school. When time allowed we would go into 'Jack's Café' on Gladstone Road to warm ourselves by the huge, open fire and have tea and toast sat underneath a poster advertising Rowntree's Elect Cocoa. Jack's toast was cut very thick and smothered in 'Maggie Ann' and reminded me of the slices Archie used to cut for himself when he visited us. Oh, when was it now! I got tips off the customers and did not tell my mum about it, deceitful but profitable and it helped to make life bearable on those cold, frosty mornings when ones fingers froze, turned blue and stuck to the bottles. I would put my hands under the hot tap on arrival at school which was excruciatingly painful and probably a stupid thing to do, but I had to get the feeling back into them before I could do any writing.

Ernie had an exceptional singing voice, sounding just like Mario Lanza, the famous tenor, only better. He had won numerous opera singing competitions but never had the opportunity to turn 'pro' mainly because he had a very large nose, and was a bit too small anyway. My mum called him Schnozzle Durante after that well known comedian with an enormous hooter. This was a bit unkind considering she had robbed him blind for years! The practice of having extra milk on the free stopped after I went to work for him and maybe it was to save me embarrassment but I was never sure. I got to keep a shilling out of the ten that Ernie paid plus my tips and thought myself lucky. I enjoyed the milk round so much, I would have done it for nothing.

The paper round in the evening was hateful. Mr. Spalding was just like Peter Lorre and I did not like Peter Lorre. He was a religious freak (Spalding not Lorre) who spent most of his time quoting the scriptures and handing out betting tips for the nags. He was a founder member of the Holy Mission on Lower Road, and on one occasion even talked me into joining their Sunday School. What he did not know was I had inside information they were going on a trip to Southport that summer in chartered buses supplied by the local bus company, which had somewhat influenced my decision. Tony Bream who was in my class at day school had gleaned the information from his dad, an inspector at the bus depot. My enjoyment of the trip was somewhat tarnished by the fact that I had to sit upstairs next to Eugene Peanut, (I never knew his real name) a teacher of the Gospel, who passed wind every time the bus went over bump and the road was full of bumps! The buses in those days were not sprung to the same comforting standard we enjoy today, so one felt every bump and smelled every trump.

Eugene was a huge man, well over six feet tall, a goodly height then, and had a voice like a nutmeg grater. They told me when he sang the hymns at the Holy Mission on a

Sunday there was always a space like a halo around where he stood. Apparently, every high note was accompanied by a rip roarer that brought tears to the eyes. After my experience on the Southport trip, I could well believe it.

Peter Lorre paid me five bob a week for carting the evening papers to those who were too idle to get off their backsides and collect their own. One of the houses on my delivery round was guarded by an oversized Alsatian called Arnold who would not let me into the garden. Despite having asked numerous times for this man eater to be locked up during delivery hour, this request had either been ignored or misunderstood. A twelve year old paper boy against an untamed, demented, sadistic barbarian like Arnold just didn't seem fair.

I brought the paper back undelivered to Peter Lorre on more than one occasion to be told I was soft and should stand up to adversity the same way as David, in the bible, had stood up to that big geezer with one eye. That was Peter Lorre for you, a complete crank. I suggested he get in touch with Humphrey Bogart, drag him out of Casablanca and see if the two of them could find a way of getting passed this sentinel. He did not seem to know what I was talking about.

One day I was delivering to Arnold's house and he was nowhere to be seen. In I went with all the bravado of a D Day invader and stuck the paper through the letter box. On turning to make my exit I saw him. He was standing at the gate. Where the hell had he sprung from! I could not even begin to guess because my mind was on other more urgent matters, like how do I get out of here! Arnold had decided I was not going to, not in one piece anyway, as his top lip was curled back in a 'look at my nice big teeth' pose. Sweat broke out on my forehead and something was trying to escape from the chest part of my shirt, and something else out of my pants. There was a horrible rumbling sound coming from Arnold's throat and all my, "Nice boy Arnold," whimpering did nothing to relieve his obvious dissatisfaction at having me standing at his front door.

There was only one option left for me as Arnold was advancing in a crouched stance, albeit only slowly. I had to shout for help. I opened my mouth but nothing came out, then tried again with the same negative result. The third attempt came out so loud it made even me jump and I knew it was coming.

"*Help, help*," I howled, and all the birds shot off the trees as though the world was coming to an end. Mine was because Arnold had not been as impressed as the birds, but I was not frightened of the birds. They could have stayed. I was frightened of Arnold. He was still edging his way towards me with that menacing look on his ugly mug. I yelled again with all my might and was on the verge of collapse when the front door behind me opened and a dirty looking man in a string vest demanded to know what all the 'bloody noise was about.' Why hadn't I thought to knock on the door or ring the bell? It seems so obvious now but when faced with certain death the straightforward thing to do is not always so defined. On seeing Arnold he burst out laughing. "He won't hurt you. He's as gentle as a new born lamb," this moron told me. "You might know that and I might know that, but he most certainly doesn't," I bellowed at this cretin who had by now taken hold of his 'little pet' and was stroking it's neck.

I never delivered to that house again telling Peter Lorre

if he insisted I would pack the job in. Five shillings a week was scant reward for facing the Hound of the Baskervilles and I was not prepared to do it. Whilst never wishing ill on any living creature before in my life, I hoped that fanged toothed fiend caught leprosy. The string vested grinning idiot who owned it had to collect his own paper from that time on.

***

The time was ripe for me to have my own bicycle, as our John's, the one I was borrowing to do the paper round, was not exactly suitable. For a start, like Graham's moustache, it had dropped handlebars, not best designed for carrying a bag full of evening papers. It was a little too big for me even with the seat fully lowered and it was painted red. I did not like bikes that were painted red, so I told my mum it was about time I had my own. Well I did not exactly tell her, one did not *tell* my mum anything. One sort of suggested it might be a good idea.

"*He who expecteth never receiveth,*" she stated in her inimitable fashion. Mum often used that proverb about all sorts of things but lord knows where she got it from. She insisted it was written in the Bible but having spoken to countless number of theologians I have never found its origin. There are similar adages, but not quite the same wording. I strongly suspect it was her own creation and a way of switching blame from her to the Almighty for something for which she was not prepared to pay without being accused of being stingy.

"There's nothing wrong with our John's," she insisted.

There were a number of things wrong with our John's, mainly it was not mine and had no rear mudguard which meant every time it rained my back had a streak of wet mud running down the middle of it. But when mum made up her mind neither a pack of wild horses nor Arnold on Park Avenue would make her budge.

Gormless Gregory had always wanted to do a paper round but none of the newsagents were daft enough to give him a job. Like John the Baptist his name had gone before him, but John had a big advantage over Gregory, he was honest. Mr. Clelland had tried to be a good Christian on one occasion but found Gregory could not lift the paper bag, and that is before the papers were put into it. On checking his stock later on Mr Clelland found that he was missing a box of Black Magic chocolates.

Gregory sometimes accompanied me on my round but I never let him anywhere near the papers. The chances are he would have nicked a couple and sold them at half price on Upshaw Station. He had a new bike he said his mum had bought on the 'never never' from Jack Bingham's on Station Road. A few bob deposit and a few bob a week and you were the proud owner of a new bike. He asked what my mum had said when I broached the subject of a bike of my own to replace our John's old racer. I told him she had said, "*He who expecteth never receiveth.*" Looking at me quizzically he said, "What the hell does that mean?" I said I did not know but she said it all the time. Broadly speaking it meant no new bike!

However, this talk of purchase on the 'never never' had set the seeds of thought in progress and I decided to approach the subject from a different direction. There is more than one way to peel a rabbit as Gregory would misquote when he was trying to be clever. What if I paid for a new bike myself out of my milk and paper round money. What would be the objection to that. To my delight and surprise, there was no objection. As long as I paid over the required amount to Bingham's every week I could go ahead but mum would have to sign for it, of course, me being under age.

For the foreseeable future my toffee ration had to be forgotten about until my bike had been paid for. This I did not mind in the least, being the proud owner of a brand new straight handlebar, blue bicycle with shiny wheels and three speed Stormy Archer gears. Our John could stuff his bike where the monkeys stuff their nuts, I did not need it any more. The only down side was that I had no alternative but to keep working at my paper and milk rounds until the bike was paid for, but that I could manage.

That Raleigh bike was cleaned every week and was my pride and joy until I left home to join the RAF when I was fifteen. On my first leave home from the air force the bike had disappeared and I never did find out where it vanished to. I was afforded an explanation with reference to it being stolen, but it all became to complicated and to much bother and I let the matter drop. I would soon be too big for it anyway, I reasoned.

***

Anyone who says schooldays are the happiest days of your life is either lying or round the twist. I hated mine and could not get away quick enough. To me they were a complete waste of time, time which could have been spent doing something useful, like shipbuilding or grand prix racing.

I learned very little at school apart from how to read and write. Simple arithmetic was easy enough, already knowing how to add and subtract by doing my mum's shopping, or messages as we called them, and woe betide me if I did not bring home the correct change. It was O.K. to bring home too much, but too little was a grave error.

Algebra, the branch of mathematics using symbols to represent unknown numbers was as mysterious to me as the far side of the moon. Why use symbols, why not just use the numbers that were there! If they were unknown numbers then how could you give them symbols anyway! This was never satisfactorily explained to me by any teacher. I also thought it would take up too much room in my brain, room that could be put to better use, so I did not bother to much about learning it.

Logarithm; the exponent indicating the power to which a fixed number, the base, must be raised to obtain a given number or variable. Pardon! What on earth were they talking about! Everyone seemed to be talking in mumbo jumbo and I decided not to join in. Technical drawing; the basic technique of draughtsmanship and architecture. O.K. if you were Christopher Wren or could do algebra and logarithms, and I think that is where I came in on that one.

Geography; this was alright because they showed us films of the natives in Africa and big ships taking cargo to foreign parts. It was much more interesting to see how other people lived than to know what $x+y=3@$ 7/6 a pound meant! Knowing such junk as 'pi r squared' could give you a brain tumour anyway, and I knew this because I had heard my dad telling our Daisy.

Music was different. One did not have to use so much brain power (and I did not have a lot) and Mr. Crossley, the teacher, was a bit weird anyway, and I liked weirdo's. He stood about six feet five inches, was almost bald and always wore a dark blue pinstriped suit, stained down both lapels with what looked like black ink. It was not unusual for him to wear odd shoes and when he sat down and crossed his legs one could see the holes in the underside of his footwear. This was the cause of many a giggling session but god help you if he caught you at it. He had a size eleven gym shoe to be used unmercifully on the backside of any miscreant, whacked out to the rhythm of the Blue Danube. Strauss was one of his favourite composers and I joined him in his admiration of the greatest writer of waltz music the world has known.

Mr. Crossley introduced me to Wolfgang Amadeus Mozart, not personally because he died in 1791, but spiritually. My appreciation of Mozart's music started back there in that classroom and has never left me. Gilbert and Sullivan also assailed our ears much to the chagrin of my peers who hated every note of it and fooled around for most of the lesson, behind Crossley's back of course. I loved every octave, semibreve and 'Air on a G String' of it but did not dare admit for loss of street cred or ridicule, as one was not supposed to like such things at that age.

Trips to Manchester were arranged to listen to the Halle Orchestra in the Free Trade Hall or to visit the Opera House for a production of one of G & S's comic operettas such as The Pirates of Penzance or The Mikado, but I was never allowed to partake. I had expressed a wish to go on many occasions only to be told by my mum that, "*He who expecteth never receiveth,*" and "*Waste of money.*" She thought the nags were a far better way to rid oneself of unwanted coins of the realm. Quite honestly, I do not know anybody who ever did go on one of these jaunts. Mr. Crossley probably went on his own.

Sport, of course, was my favourite at school and I always looked forward to the games periods. There was nothing more depressing than to have a game of either football or cricket called off because the teacher delegated to take the lesson did not want to get wet. We would have played in a monsoon, but the teachers were not prepared to get rained on just to please us. A good dousing never hurt anyone, was my philosophy, but that counted for nothing. I was the only one of our gang who played sports at school, the rest were either cleverer and did things like algebra and trigonometry or were denser like Gormless Gregory and did gardening all day. Far from being the happiest days of my life, school for me was a drag, a dreaded burden one had to put up with until one was old enough to leave and join the real world where nobody made you do things that did not make sense!!

***

In the fifties, third rate French films were all the rage and as teenagers we would travel as far as Eccles, Stretford or even All Saints in Manchester, a goodly distance, just to see them. It was the thought of doing something daring that attracted us the most, but a lot of kids were strictly forbidden from going. I was never forbidden because no one in my family ever knew I was going, or if they did, they were unconcerned. Therefore, I had to tell the gang what had gone on, or more like it, what had come off. The films were always 'tripe' and we could not understand a word being said but that did not matter. They were French and that was the attraction.

The 'flea pit' in Upshaw, or The Palace as it was so aptly named, was situated on Kings Road opposite the market and showed every bit of trash ever produced. The building that housed the cinema was grand but sadly no longer exists. One such film called 'Isle of Levant' was about nudists prancing around on an island somewhere in the Mediterranean.

I can not think why the name of this film has remained with me but it has. It was absolute junk, but a must for any French film voyeur. Not a word of English was spoken throughout the entire film and the only reason I stayed until the end was so I could boast about it at school the next day. That is my story anyway. There were women showing their 'diddies' and other things whilst playing tennis, and women's 'diddies' were big time for us young boys. How sad! However, I was now the expert and had to answer many questions from my school mates.

Gormless Gregory was with me on this trip. In fact, I think he paid for the tickets, and some scruff from Stretford whose name I never knew joined us. He was a cousin or some such thing of Gregory and I only ever saw him at French films. He was probably uglier and cheekier than Gregory, had a habit of picking his nose, was a thoroughly despicable character and I hated him on sight. I think he was eventually sent to Borstal where young offenders were sent to be straightened out.

The Palace was to take a clobbering in the Teddy Boy era when rock ' n' roll first hit the scene with such films as Rock Around the Clock, The Girl Can't Help It, and Rock, Rock, Rock. Cinemas took the brunt of the hysteria with the seats being smashed and slashed open with flick knives, the curse of the period, and jive dancing was enacted down the aisles whilst general mayhem ensued. It was a far cry from the innocence of French Nudist films.

I attended all the rock films to visit our local picture houses and witnessed much of the destruction that took place, but never felt it necessary to smash or bust up anything. I valued other people's property too much to get involved, and anyway, I might have got caught.

***

13

When I was about eight I was a member of the 8th Upshaw Cub Pack and had been hopelessly in love with Akela, the pack leader. Akela translates roughly to Den Mother but she was more like a lover than a mother as far as I was concerned. I started young. She would have been about thirty five at the time but I was convinced she was head over heels in love with me.

I never progressed to the Scouts which was the normal way of things as my dad said all scoutmasters were poofs, and no son of his was going to summer camp with a gang of willy woofters. He was wrong of course. However, he held no such illusions about the leader of the local Air Training Corps Squadron which I joined when I was twelve. One was supposed to be thirteen by law but who was going to check on you, or even care. As long as you didn't look too young and said you were thirteen, you were in.

Flight Lieutenant Watson was the squadron commander and he was hardly the type one would fall in love with. Although a nice bloke, he had a presence about him that made one stand back and listen to what he had to say. He ran a strict outfit and would stand for no nonsense. Jim Clements, Gormless Gregory and myself all joined at the same time but Gregory's membership was not to last for long. Firstly, they could not find a uniform to fit him. The ones with extra material at the back to accommodate a hump had apparently all been used up. Secondly, he could not march properly and kept tripping people up, which got right up the nose of the drill instructor, a big lad who went to Manchester Grammar School and did not like to be messed about. Thirdly, he knew nothing about aircraft and had no intention of learning.

On his last attendance Gormless tried to filch an e-flat trumpet but was caught by the drill instructor who thumped his ear hole and threw him out into the lane. He was witnessed running down the lane away from the squadron hut shouting that he did not like the Air Force anyway and was going to join the army cadets. He tried but the army would not have him either.

My first flight with the ATC was in an old Avro Anson world war two light bomber, taking to the air from RAF Woodvale near Southport. The airfield had originally been built as a fighter base to protect Liverpool but was now used almost exclusively as a training camp for cadets. This was the first time I had ever been airborne and it was to have a lasting effect on me. The sheer wonder of seeing Blackpool tower from above instead of from below was pure magic and was one of the reasons for my enlistment into the RAF a few years later. All of a sudden Oscar Wilde's stars did not seem so far away and I was beginning to see how that swamp could be drained.

Jim Clements was with me on this trip but paid more

attention to the wild birds that had taken up residence around the airfield. Whilst we sat on the peri-track which surrounded the aerodrome listening to the instructor, Jim was posed, notebook in hand, scribbling for all he was worth. The instructor thought he was the keenest cadet amongst us to be taking notes of all he was being told about the various aircraft in service. What Jim was actually doing was drawing the birds in their natural environment, no doubt to appear on our school notice board at some future date. The worm.

Two seater Chipmonk trainer aircraft were a great favourite of the cadets and many happy hours were spent pretending to be fighter pilots. I visited RAF Halton near Aylesbury, the home of the RAF Apprentices, and this really got the blood tingling. The public relations team of the RAF left no stone unturned when it came to convincing volatile, impressionable, young lads that a career in air force blue was the life for them.

It was in the cadets I learned to play the drums and the trumpet, attaining the exalted position of leading drummer and later of leading trumpeter in the corps band. The leading drummer was given a silver coloured drum to denote he was far superior to the rest of the mob who had to make do with brass ones that had to be 'bulled up' with Brasso. The leading trumpeter played a silver trumpet whilst the mere mortals had brass ones that required the same cleaning treatment as the drums. I was very proud of this achievement as it had never been done before, and I do not know if it has been done since. Being able to play these instruments was to be beneficial to me later on when I joined the RAF, enabling me to escape aircraft guard duty on occasions due to band practice, which appeared to take precedence over most other activities. I believe the 'Dam Busters' raid was postponed for two days due to band practice!

William Danson, who lived not far from me, was a member of the same cadet squadron and would call on parade nights to walk the mile or so to the squadron HQ. On occasions, youths called across the road to us with words I had never heard before, like 'wog' and 'coon' and other expressions not in my vocabulary. I did not know if these remarks were aimed at William or me. In my ignorance I thought they might have had some connection to the uniform we were wearing. William said to take no notice. He was a couple of years older than me but we got on very well together. We had played football and cricket and had some good fun on Golden Hill Park, but I had never known him to get upset about anything before and this name calling knocked him out of his stride.

I had not realised William was of Indian descent and had an Asian appearance. Having never previously come across colour prejudice I had not noticed he was 'coloured'. This had to be pointed out to me and it took a long time before it sunk in that some people looked upon dark skinned people with disdain. My ignorance of such things was huge, but sometimes ignorance is bliss. In my eyes William was William and no different from me and I could not make sense of it all. He was a nice guy and remained my friend until the time I left home and lost contact with him.

***

After a couple of years, I decided I had gone as far as I could in the air cadets and decided to try something new. How about the army cadets that had given Gormless such short shrift? I knew a couple of the lads from school who were members and had enjoyed summer camp in the Welsh countryside which sounded O.K. to me. I arrived at Folton Barracks full of misgivings because I knew the incumbent caretaker, Regimental Sergeant Major Robert Smethurst, who was an acquaintance of my dad, and was more biting than acid drops. In fact, he was well-known throughout the entire area for his loud voice and his meticulous appearance whenever he strode through HIS town. He paraded the streets as if he actually owned them and I do not recall anybody ever disputing this with him.

Only a small man in stature, but what he lacked in height he made up for in presence. He always wore grey trousers and a navy blue blazer, a Royal Artillery badge proudly displayed on the breast pocket, a pair of folded yellow gloves carried in his right hand and a overcoat of indefinable style folded neatly and carried over his left arm. He sported a pencil line moustache and his hair parted down the middle, held in place with Brylcreem.

The barracks had a large area of ground surrounding it. This included a parade square and a vehicle parking area which backed onto the army garages and workshops. It was encircled by low iron railings and gates that were usually open, but no kids ever ventured into this holy ground to play, having more sense than to incur the wrath of R.S.M. Smethurst. It is hard to see how such a small man could instil such fear, not only to us kids, but to grown ups as well who paid him the highest reverence.

The cadet force was commanded by Major Livingstone, a huge man who was always laughing and teasing the lads about one thing or another. He asked me if I had belonged to any other youth organisation, so he could check me out, but I lied and said no. This was because I had told the air cadets I was leaving due to our family going to join Cousin Martha in Australia. I thought this was the best thing to do at the time because the air cadets did not like to lose members and tried to talk you out of 'bailing out', presumably to protect their own status and prestige as youth leaders.

Being accepted into the 46 Royal Ordinance Corps Cadet Force, necessitated me exchanging my air force blue for khaki. I asked Major Livingstone why he had rejected Gormless Gregory because I had spotted a lot of ungainly, ugly, undersized cadets in the company, and I did not believe the story that Gregory had put around about himself being too small. The Major said part of cadet training involved .22 rifle shooting in the indoor range on the upper floor of the barracks, and he did not feel it was a good idea to put a firearm in the hands of one who was so clumsy, ham-fisted and maladroit as Gregory. I could not find fault with this reasoning and was impressed at the speed at which Gormless had been rumbled.

The barracks was the home of the local Territorial Army and the cadets were part of their set up. Summer camps were spent together and many a 'rum do' was to be had with these rogues who paid scant regard to the law when it came to under age drinking. The cadets wore ACF flashes on the shoulder of their tunics which, of course, stood for Army Cadet Force. On summer camp, however, it stood for Army Catering Force and we strode into the pubs with our big brothers in the Terriers pretending to be regular soldiers. Most of the time we were thrown out on our ears with the grown up soldiers being told that they should know better, but on occasions we were hidden away in the corner and sat down with our backs to the bar before the landlord caught sight of us. The Terriers did the waiter service for us, paid for our refreshments and 'escorted' us back to our tents after a splendid evening out. The headaches on the firing range the next morning were not so splendid, however, and neither was the Montezuma's revenge we all experienced as a result of our felonious binges.

Every Christmas, the Territorial Army officers of our region held a grand party, and one particular year it was the turn of our barracks to provide the venue. We cadets were offered the job of helping out in the kitchen and clearing up the remnants of foodstuff the officers could not manage to stow away. Numerous pieces of turkey and Christmas puddings were returned to the Army Catering Corps lackeys who provided the fare. The turkey tasted delicious and the pudding was divine. Half full glasses of sherry and other varieties of alcoholic drink, mostly unknown to me, were returned to the kitchen to be thrown down the sink and washed away. Much of it was washed down our juvenile throats whilst the army staff were not looking and before long the kitchen and surrounding area started to become decidedly divorced from reality. It was like the whole world had suddenly started to spin at an incredible rate and I do not remember being of much help to anyone that night, but I do know that I felt undeniably ill the next morning.

One summer we spent a few days with the Army Junior Leaders Unit, Royal Artillery, at their base at Hereford, later to be taken over by the SAS. We were billeted in the old world war two Nissen huts, twenty two of us in each, and great fun was to be had after 'lights out' at nine thirty p.m. All sorts of boyish pranks were enacted and challenges were the order of the day, or night in this case. One night we dared one of the cadets to run naked twice around the parade square, which was '*SACRED GROUND*' and not to be trifled with. The parade square was about one hundred yards away from our hut but clearly visible to us because it was lit up with arc lights at night and nothing obstructed our view. It must have been about eleven o'clock when, entering into the spirit of things and not wishing to be thought of as chicken, the challenge was accepted by a kid from Wythenshawe, and before long he was wishing he was back there. The rain was lashing down and it was not particularly warm as this idiot set off on his bare arsed run, shouting, "*Geronimo*" as he sped down the whitewash lined road leading to the square.

Without further ado, all the doors to the billet were securely locked and all the windows closed. We crowded the window space shouting encouragement and rude remarks to the only one of us who had any bottle, he who was getting drenched to the skin and probable pneumonia in the process, as he galloped around the drill square gleaming in the glow of the arc lights and then vanishing into the shadow beyond. He arrived back panting and laughing, standing there in nothing more than his army issue boots, and, no doubt, looking forward to a nice warm bed awaiting him inside the billet. His grinning face slowly changed to a look of consternation and panic as he realised he was locked out and nobody was prepared to let him in.

After what must have seemed an eternity to this divested moron from Wythenshawe, but was in reality about fifteen minutes, we decided enough was enough and, seeing as he was freezing his nuts off, had better let him in. But 'too late' was the famous cry. The orderly corporal had spotted him and was heading in our direction. Orderly corporals are not renowned for their humour, due to the fact that they would rather be in the NAAFI swilling pints with their mates than tramping around in the dark making sure the camp was secure. This corporal was no exception and placed the lot of us on officer's report, to be dealt with at nine o'clock the following morning. Luckily for us the C.O. had a sense of humour and thought the whole thing was hilarious. However, he had to back up his corporal so sentenced us to attend field gun parade later that morning. This had been on our schedule anyway, and he knew it, so we got off without punishment.

Field gun parade consisted, for us cadets anyway, of standing behind the Junior Leaders and watching them go through the routine of loading, unloading and the various drill routines that went with ceremonial drill with the 22 pounder field gun. After watching for about half an hour, with fascination, to the procedure taking place on the same parade ground so graciously galloped around by our friend the night before, we were treated to a finale some of us will never forget. Unknown to us, the troop had loaded a blank shell up the breech of the 22 pounder. The order rang out, as we had heard for the last half hour, "Stand back. Range. Aim. FIRE". Usually a click was heard as the firing pin struck an empty chamber. This time, the loudest bang this side of hell assaulted our ears as we stood no more than two yards behind the weapon. Two cadets fell over with fright, all of us jumped out of our skin but the worst affected was a kid from Shropshire who filled his pants and ran off in the direction of the billet crying his eyes out.

Later that day the Troop Lieutenant gathered us together to wish us bon voyage back to our respective units. He said he had ordered the 'big bang' to teach us a lesson or two and hoped it had registered. Firstly, never become complacent about anything. Secondly, never take anything on face value and be ready for the unexpected events life would undoubtedly throw at us. Thirdly as his way of saying, "Don't mess with my parade ground." I think his point was taken.

***

14

A carrot topped lass called Margaret Ashworth lived across the road from me in the upholsterer's shop, or more precisely at the back and over it. I had known her since infant school, though she was a year in front of me and not really allowed to play with us rough boys. She came to play with us thanks to Anne Hilton, a girl who lived in the avenue at the end of our entry whose garden backed onto our square and was a friend of hers. Anne's elder brother would eventually marry my sister Daisy.

We all grew up together and spent many wonderful innocent hours in each other's company. Margaret's dad was the local upholsterer and furniture supplier, a member of the Chamber of Trade and a pillar of society in the Upshaw area. He was very protective and kept a close watch on her activities. He was one of the very few people in the area to own a telephone and a car, an Austin Ten, which was a problem at times because we never knew where he would turn up. If he saw her with me she would be in trouble, but he need not have worried because Maggie, as she became later in life, was as clean living and moral as they come and really gave no cause for concern, as indeed I myself.

She was an only child (Oh, how I envied that) who took piano lessons and knew nothing about bookies and betting shops or lighting fires in old iron grates. This never made her stuck up or act in a superior way. In fact, on the contrary, she was a joy to be with and longed to be a member of a large family herself, being envious of me! She still had a lot to learn.

There was always a feeling of closeness between Maggie and me, nothing really tangible, but more a feeling of understanding and trust. The contemporary term would be sole mates and that is exactly what we were. Even so, I can never remember a time when I was not in love with her, even when very young, and could never envisage a time when I would not be. We both felt we were destined to spend the rest of our lives together, and these thoughts, which were not always silent, were somewhat prophetic, but not without a rather lengthy hiatus.

She attended the Baptist Church and was usually in the Christmas Pantomime and various other stage productions they enacted from time to time. I became a member of her church and it's youth club so we could spend more time together, go places and generally have fun without the fear of her dad showing up. She came to the Air Cadets Christmas Dance, along with Anne Hilton and Len Jackson, and we passed a wonderful dreamy evening smooching to Elvis and the Platters, that marvellous black harmony group whose sound emanated straight from heaven. What excuse she used to be out so late I cannot imagine but the evening is remembered as one full of bliss and contentment. What joy young love is, how utterly carefree and intoxicating.

Maggie had a wonderful bubbly personality that endeared her to people and made it impossible to dislike her. As a teenager she was full of energy and gusto, hyperactive one might say, and her great energy and drive was put to the best possible use. She, along with Anne, Lynn Green, Wendy Thompson and occasionally Carol Booth who was not really from our area but went to the same school as Maggie, gave concerts to old folk who were slowly dying of boredom in nursing homes in the locality, and these were received with great appreciation. They sang songs from the music halls, popular at that time, and comedy routines that at least the old people thought were funny, and this, after all, was the object of the exercise. Maggie and Lynn did a double act calling themselves the Maralyn Sisters and it went down a treat in the various homes they performed in.

Lynn, like Maggie, was an effervescent character and delightful company who had that quality of making one feel completely at ease. Once again, it would be very hard to dislike her even if one tried, though I doubt anyone ever did.

One school holiday, the Baptist Church arranged an outing to Nether Alderley, a select area of Cheshire, with field games the order of the day. Before the games in the meadow, we were taken around a quaint flour mill that was still operating and shown how the whole thing worked. It was fascinating, though not as much fun as Maggie and I had walking through the woods afterwards. We decided that field games were for the younger ones and a botanical experience was more to our liking. Along with a few other teenagers we spent a cracking afternoon amongst the trees in complete innocence, holding hands and the occasional 'smacker' being enough to satisfy our desires. The promiscuous age had not yet arrived and I know for sure if it had we would not have been party to it. My feelings of love and respect for Maggie were such that I could not have marred it by trying to be more intimate than we were. She would not have let me anyway, or anyone else come to that!

Maggie's teenage years were not all a bed of roses having to put up with an over protective father who at times made life somewhat difficult for her. In his own way he was doing what he thought best, for he loved his daughter very much, but where does protection end and suffocation begin! Often we had to dodge down an entry when we saw his car approaching, and albeit good fun at times, it eventually became wearing. She once said to me, " No matter what happens Fred Harris, I know for certain that one day I will marry you." - Maggie and I split up about eighteen months after I entered the RAF.

***

As far as teddy boys went, Gormless Gregory was not a very good one. The lump on his back did not help and being undersized was a positive hindrance. His lack of presence and 'back alley' clothing was not something that accorded well with the teds concept, so he did not really fit the bill. For those too young to remember, the teddy boys appeared in the mid-fifties and were a youth cult who wore mock Edwardian fashions, such as tight narrow trousers and long jackets with velvet collars. The shoes were either pointed and known as winkle pickers or wide with crepe soles, commonly referred to as brothel creepers. They wore boot lace ties and socks of fluorescent pink or green, or any other colour that would shock. Their hair was thick and greased and long sideburns featured down either side of their face. The front of the hair was combed forward like an elephant's trunk and the back brought together to present the image of the rear end of a duck and was known as a D.A.. Often called teds for short, many of them thought of themselves as tough or delinquent, but Gormless just did not fit the image no matter how hard he tried. The teds appeared with the advent of rock 'n' roll music and the two were intrinsically linked.

Gregory would hang around the Willow Milk Bar on Gladstone Road or the Rose Bud on Upshaw Bridge, regular meeting places for the teds, although he was not really old enough to be one of them. John O'Sullivan and I often went along and spent the entire afternoon sipping one coke between the two of us. How the milk bars ever made money is beyond my imagination as nobody ever spent anything. They just sat around talking and listening to music. The juke box always made a good living by being played continuously throughout the day, and often well into the evening.

Elvis Presley; Bill Haley; Chuck Berry; The Platters; Freddie Bell and the Bell Boys; Little Richard; Cliff Richard and the Shadows; Billy Fury; Frankie Limeman and the Teenagers; Slim Whitman; Connie Francis; Brenda Lee; the list of singers was endless and their records were played over and over again at a tanner a go.

There was one teddy boy who frequented the Willow

Milk Bar and was a hero figure to Gormless who hung on his every word, most of them unintelligible. This fitted in well with his own limited vocabulary. I never knew where this latter-day hero lived but his name was Nixon and Gormless referred to him, behind his back, of course, as 'The Sacramento Teddy Boy'. Only Gormless knew the reason for this and he was not for telling. He certainly did not live in Sacramento, but Gormless would not know that, probably thinking Sacramento was somewhere near Old Trafford football ground. I often saw Sacramento selling flowers to visitors outside Cottage Hospital main gates, and a roaring trade he did, although where he got his flowers from I never knew. The graveyard was not far away!

The teddy boys held frequent battles with gangs from other areas like Irlam, Stretford and Eccles and these hostilities were a thing to avoid if it was at all possible. I encountered one such skirmish on Upshaw Bridge between the Upshaw and Irlam teds that escalated down Station Road and into Gladstone Road where the Willow Milk Bar took the full impact of the assault. The windows were put through and the seats and tables smashed to smithereens before the police arrived to restore order.

The favourite weapons were flick knives, knuckle dusters and bicycle chains with no quarter asked and none given when warfare began. Nobody ever knew what they were fighting about and nobody ever cared. It was all so crazy in the same barking mad way that cinemas were wrecked. Some said it was a protest but did not know what the protest was. Others were just plain stupid and violent. Come the mid-1960s, the teddy boy had had his day and a new species had taken over, or rather two breeds, the

'Mods' and the 'Rockers'. They too would have their battles but that comes somewhat out of the parameter of my story and had no bearing on my early life.

***

Synchronous with the teddy boys and rock'n'roll went skiffle music, or skuffle as it was originally known by the Americans in the early 1900's. This was a style of informal, popular good time music played chiefly on guitars and home-made improvised percussion instruments. Such as wash-tub or tea chest bass, whereby a hole was made in the bottom of the tub or chest and a piece of string put through and knotted to prevent it being pulled out. The other end of the sting was attached to an old brush stave which would be pulled taught against the chest and, hey presto, by slackening and tightening the stave a very effective bass instrument was created.

Another improvised instrument was a hair comb with a piece of paper wrapped around it played like a mouth organ. A fiddle could be made out of an old cigar box or shoe box, and mother's galvanised wash-board strummed with a couple of thimbled fingers was just the job. An old jug to blow into created a very satisfying sound (thus Jug Band) and a kazoo, a cigar shaped instrument made of metal or plastic, with a membranous diaphragm of thin paper that vibrated with nasal sounds when the musician hummed into it, which could be bought at Woolworths for about a tanner, rounded off the group.

The music played by these bands was a mixture of American folk, tin pan alley, blues and music hall played as pop. The early exponents of skiffle were American black people such as Blind Lemon Jefferson, Will Ezell, The Hokum Boys and many others. These musicians had to improvise with what they could find to make music as the early part of the twentieth century did not bless them with the cash needed to purchase ready-made orthodox instruments, and so the movement was born. The kids on the streets of New Orleans took this music to their hearts, so mother's kitchen utensils disappeared and re-appeared in the guise of percussion instruments which gave a great deal more pleasure than the purpose for which they were originally intended.

The introduction of skiffle into our back entry did not come from any of the American originals' however, but from across the Scottish border by way of Lonnie Donegan, a banjo player in Chris Barber's Jazz Band. Lonnie made a record of a song called 'Rock Island Line', a macho piece of music which, of course, appealed to the teddy boys and consequently sold over three million copies. He became an instant star and went on to record such numbers as 'Putting on the Style', 'My Old Man's a Dustman' and 'Grand Coulee Dam'. Everything he recorded seemed to be a hit.

Chas and Kerry McDevitt then appeared on the skiffle scene with their gritty blend of jazz, gospel and blues and attracted huge crowds. Shirley Douglas joined the band and added an even bigger sex appeal, and I, of course, fell instantly in love with her. Then along came a young lady from Leicester called Nancy Whiskey and joined Chas and Shirley. *Wow!* This was all getting too much. I didn't know which one to be in love with so I stopped bothering. There was no way I would be able to get them down our back entry anyway, so what was the point. Nancy Whiskey became known as the 'Queen of Skiffle' and had an enormous hit, along with the Chas Mcdevitt Skiffle Group, with a song called 'Freight Train'. It sold millions of copies and remained in the charts for months. Nancy left Chas McDevitt in 1957 and formed her own skiffle group with Diz Disley and Bob Kelly.

There I lost track of them but enough seeds had been sown to encourage me to start my own skiffle group. Gormless Gregory had a guitar, the one he had supposedly stolen from King Street, and the rest would be easy. Don and Skiver were all for the idea and could supply some of the instruments required. Their mums' kitchens, they said, were laden with utensils which they were sure would not be missed. None of us could sing, but what the hell, nothing ventured as they say. On asking Gregory how well he could play the guitar, he said he had mastered three chords. I told him that was two more than would be required so that was alright.

I suggested Skiver could have a word with his mate Mr. Lampton, the chandler, who had so graciously supplied us with nails for Kon Tiki, to see if he could provide us with a tea chest, as I had seen some in his shop holding all sorts of merchandise. Gregory said not to bother as he could steal one from the back yard of the Co-op where there were stacks of them. How he knew this I never enquired. I have said before, it was not always a good idea to know where Gregory obtained his information. I pointed out that this meant scaling a ten foot brick wall, and then getting the chest back over. Never one to be put off with such trivialities, Gregory asked me to meet him in the entry behind the Co-op after closing time and the deed would be done.

When I arrived at the rendezvous, Gormless Gregory was already there standing on an object and trying frantically to reach the top of the Co-op yard wall. He was having little success as his lack of height was a positive disadvantage when it came to scaling towering ramparts. Not only that but the object he was standing on kept tipping over and depositing Gregory on the cobbles like a sack of Jack Hobson's coal being thrown down the coal hole into our cellar. I told him to remove himself and I would climb up, being a lot taller than he, and perhaps he could then climb on my shoulders and onto the top of the wall. This we did and it wasn't long before Gregory was straddling the brick divide and grinning like a mindless moron.

"See," he said, "Told you I could do it." "Hang on a mo," I interjected and thought deeply. "Once you have dropped into the yard, how are you going to get out again?" Neither of us had thought of this. He said perhaps I could climb over and give him a bunk up in the same manner as we way had gained entry. I didn't think that was a very good idea, because I would then be stuck inside unable to climb out and would have to wait until the next morning before being released by Mr. Jackson, the manager, who would not be best pleased.

It was then that the thing we had both been standing on to gain height tipped over and I went flat on my back. Picking myself up and placing the object back against the wall, I discovered that it was a 'tea-chest'. "You great ninny," I yelled, "Where did you get this from?" He told me it had been in his cellar for years but did not think it was good enough because it was dirty and full of spiders, and the ones in the Co-op yard were clean with nice writing on them. I could not imagine why the writing was of significance because Gormless could not read, but I let it pass. The truth was, he just liked nicking things. Never mind, we had our bass. I supplied the string required from a piece that I found wrapped around Mrs. Bradman's gate where the hinge had rusted. I was sure she would not mind, as it was being put to good use by helping us to enhance our culture so to speak. Anyway, I had no intention of telling her.

Skiver produced a kazoo he had found in his young sister's toy box, and although it was pink and not very macho, it would have to do. He also brought a colander that his mum had thrown out and we all stood looking at each other in bewilderment. Realising his mistake he shrugged and tossed the straining utensil aside. It was decided that I would play the tea-chest, Don would play the comb and the jug, a cracked old thing picked up from the local council tip. Skiver would blow the kazoo as none of us wanted to catch a disease from any saliva that remained after his sister had blown herself silly on it. Strangely, we never gave a thought of any disease that might lurk in the jug from the tip. Gregory, being the only real musician amongst us, would, of course play his guitar.

Our cellar was the appointed recording studio and all was set for our first rehearsal which we were sure would lead to greater and highly profitable times. We tried Lonnie Donegan's 'Putting on the Style', the first line being 'Putting on the agony, putting on the style'. Agony it most certainly was and my mother let us know it in no uncertain terms. The cellar door burst open and a yard brush was hurdled down the stairs in our direction followed by the words "Sod off." Skiver said we could try his cellar but didn't think his dad would allow it as he had strict house rules. Don didn't think his mum would approve as she was a member of the 'Friends of the Halle Orchestra' and did not like pop music. So it had to be Gormless Gregory and his cellar full of spiders.

As much as we persevered, our musical skills did not improve. In fact, the more we tried, the worse we got. None of us could sing a note and the sound issuing forth from our home made instruments was nothing short of torture. Gregory with his guitar was the only one with any sort of rhythm and he soon began to leave us all behind, musically that is. He was becoming

serious about music, the first thing he had ever been serious about in his entire life, and, of course, that was the direction that his life's work would eventually lead him. So, one could say that I played a part in creating a professional musician. The rest of us decided that our fame and fortune lay in other directions and gave it up as a bad job. It was good fun whilst it lasted, that is, if you did not have to stand and listen to it.

***

15

It was a long journey to make on my own as a fifteen year old, being as I had rarely been out of my own home town without somebody to accompany me. There had been the odd occasion when I ventured forth, like visiting our Sam in Stourbridge, but nothing so adventurous as this. The Sunday School trips to Southport and Nether Alderley hardly compared to the expedition now being undertaken. Manchester to Hereford by rail was quite a challenge for me, the latter, in those days anyway, being somewhat off the beaten track so to speak. "Change at Crewe," the man had said, and I peered closely at each station name board as we entered the platform, not wanting to miss my connection or lord knows where I might have ended up.

I recall very little about the journey apart from scanning every stop to see if I had arrived. The rest was quite uneventful apart from my active mind. Cliff Richard had just recorded his hit song 'Travelling Light', and I remember thinking how very apt as I glanced at my small holdall containing washing gear, my very own, newly purchased toothbrush, a tin of tooth powder and little else.

We had been told not to bring very much as everything we required would be provided. I thought to myself, have I now managed to drain the swamp despite those alligators who were so ready to drag me under! Are the stars I have been looking at for so long now within touching distance! The RAF was the right branch of the armed forces for the stars that was for sure. Off to Hereford again, but a different camp to the one that provided so much fun for me as an army cadet. I was bound for the RAF Station this time and it was for real, not just kid's stuff. This camp was another later to be taken over by the SAS.

It was towards the end of 1959, at two-thirty in the afternoon, when the west country equivalent of 'Puffin' Billy' pulled into Hereford railway station. There I was greeted by a drill sergeant holding a clip board with a sheet of paper attached to it, on which were written scores of names. As I alighted the train, he approached me and asked ever so politely if I was one of the lads who had come to join the RAF Boy Entrant School. I told him I was, to which he replied at the top of his voice, "Well don't just stand there looking stupid, get fell in over there with them other teddy boys."

Welcome to your new life I thought, but all the bawling and shouting did not bother me as much as some of the other recruits because I had been in the air and army cadets and knew roughly what to expect. Teddy boy I was not, but to the drill sergeant anybody under the age of thirty not in a uniform was a teddy boy. One or two of our number were indeed teds but all that would soon change. Before long the greased elephant's trunk and DA hair styles would be transformed into the regulation short back and sides of Her Majesty's armed forces. The brothel creeper and winkle picker shoes would be ousted as far as the drill sergeant could throw them and hob nailed boots would take their place. This was just one of the many shocks to the system that awaited the next entry of Boy Entrants into the RAF. 'Per Ardua Ad Astra' or 'Through Difficulties to the Stars' is the motto of the RAF, and we were just about to find out how true this was.

There were over a hundred bedraggled, nervous and apprehensive youths lined up in rows of three blocking the station approach from the city of Hereford, and anyone wishing to gain entry to the platform had to negotiated a detour around this unsightly rabble. The drill sergeant then introduced himself as Sergeant Lean of the RAF and pointed out a side kick who stood to the rear of us and answered to the name of Corporal Connolly of the RAF Regiment. Any nonsense, larking about or speaking without being spoken to first, would result in swift and painful retribution from the corporal who represented the RAF at boxing, we were told.

Corporal Connolly said nothing but moved around from the back of us to come into full view and a menacing sight he was. He stood about five feet eleven inches tall, with shoulders pulled back and his back as straight as a broom handle. He presented a beautifully broken nose, no doubt a memento of his activities in the boxing ring, and a presence that defied challenge. His arms were placed behind his back which made his chest stick out and his highly polished uniform buttons glistened in the wintery sunshine. The highly buffed peak of his service cap had been slashed to give it a downward slope, in the fashion of a guardsman, requiring the wearer to hold his head back in order to see properly. The 'bulled' toe caps of his boots were good enough to use as a shaving mirror and his blanco'd webbing belt rounded off an immaculate turn out.

The area around us was beginning to fill up with uniformed boy entrants from RAF Hereford going home on leave for half term. The uniforms thrilled me and I could not wait to receive mine. I hoped I would be issued with a cap like Corporal Connolly's with a sloping peak and not one of the stick-out style that made the wearer look like a duck. What I did not know was that all RAF caps were the straight or stick-out peak type when issued and one had to 'doctor' them to make them look presentable. This, of course, was strictly against 'Queen's Regulations' but never stopped many of us from improving on the manufacturer's design. However, plenty obeyed QR's and looked complete prats! A fleet of RAF coaches transported us from the railway station to the RAF camp situated a few miles out of the city. When I say coaches, I use the term loosely, as these personnel carriers were one of the most uncomfortable modes of transport ever devised. It was a vehicle I would come to know very well in the years that lay ahead. The seats were hard and upright, with a short back rest, so every bump the coach went over provided a dig in the spine by the metal rim that surrounded the seat. I imagine the designer had forgotten to put springs on his blue print so the bus was built without them, or at least that is how it felt to the passengers. But as the drill sergeant said, we were not here to enjoy ourselves.

RAF Hereford began life as RAF Credenhill, the name of the area where the camp is domicile, but had changed sometime in the 1950's when it received the freedom of the city. It became No.3 School of Technical Training for RAF Boy Entrants in January, 1950, and on my arrival in 1959, still looked very much as it had done on its inauguration, with wooden billets and offices. In fact, the whole camp was built of wood and painted black, apart from the three aircraft hangers constructed of corrugated iron and steel girders. The camp cinema, or Astra as it was called, was an addition to the original camp and was brick built. All RAF stations throughout the world had a cinema called the Astra owned and operated by the RAF Kinema Corp.

On arrival at No. 3 School of Technical Training, we were lined up outside the Astra which that week was showing Kenneth More in 'Reach for the Sky', the story of

Douglas Bader, the legless RAF fighter pilot of world war two. This was just more propaganda to let us know how fortunate we were to be joining such an elite outfit, and I fully agreed with this sentiment. I did, indeed, feel privileged for a myriad of reasons. Nevertheless, this could wait because Corporal Connolly was reading out names from the clip board to which we had to answer, "Here corporal." He would then shout out the hut to which we had been allocated. Whilst waiting to be conveyed from the rail station, I had been chatting with a Scouse lad called Alan Crawford and we seemed to get on splendidly and hoped we would be billeted together.

Things like that matter sometimes and this was one of those times. I awaited for the pugilist corporal to get to the H's as everything in the RAF is done in alphabetical order. It was unfortunate for those who were called Williams or Yates as they had to take what was left after the rest had been given the pick of the litter.

Eventually he got there. "Arris ," he called, without the aitch. "Here corporal," I shouted back as loud as I could. "Arris ," he called again, looking around the raw recruits in front of him. "Here corporal," I screamed even louder. "Wake up lad. Are you deaf, daft or asleep?" There was an expletive used as well but I will leave it out for the sake of decency. I assured him I was neither deaf, daft nor asleep, (leaving out the expletive of course) and had answered him the first time. "Oh, a smart arse are we? I'll be watching you me lad," he bellowed in his broad Northern Irish accent. That was my introduction to someone who would be one of my instructors for the next eighteen months. Heavens above, what a start. "Trenchard Lines, Hut 77, at the double, go," he screamed at me as he had done to everyone who had preceded me. Good, it was the same hut as Scouse Crawford who had been called out earlier having a name, of course, beginning with C.

I picked up my small bag of belongings and dashed off in the direction indicated by my two striped instructor and found hut 77 without too much bother. There, standing in the doorway to the hut, was a small, rotund corporal who said his name was Corporal Williams and that he would be my trade instructor for the period of my training at Hereford. Corporal Connolly, he told me, was my discipline instructor who would take us for drill, small arms training and survival exercises amongst other things. "Find a bed and make yourself at home," Corporal Williams said, and left to meet the next recruit.

I liked Corporal Williams from the word go and I was never to change my opinion in the eighteen months it took him and others to turn me into an airman. Another chap popped his head through the billet door and announced himself as Corporal Stanley and said he looked after our domestic matters. He did not wait to see if we had any domestic matters which was just as well because we did not know what they were. I smiled to myself and Scouse Crawford wanted to know what I found so funny. I told him I thought it was strange the way all those mothers had given their sons the Christian name of Corporal. He obviously liked my sense of humour and we both set off into uncontrolled fits of laughter. From that moment on, Scouse Crawford and I became inseparable and were referred to as the 'terrible twins from up north'.

But not as far north as a lad who was spread-eagled on a

bed, half way down the billet. He said his name was Angus McBride and that was about all we understood of his ramblings which lasted for about five minutes. His tirade was totally incomprehensible and Scouse Crawford and I stood looking at each other with mouths wide open. There were several others in the billet who obviously shared our lack of understanding and looked from one to another for assistance. "What the hell did he say?" I enquired of the rest. "Haven't got the foggiest, but I think it was Russian," came Scouse's rejoin. "I'm Scottish, yer Sassenachs," hollered Angus and went off into another completely baffling monologue, much to the amusement of us all. "Hey Jock, grab this bed next to mine," I pleaded, for I thought I would be in need of a good laugh before very long.

***

"Get fell in outside," came the order from some unseen person standing on the road in front of hut 77. It sounded like our Northern Irish corporal who had that unmistakable twang to this voice. The delivery of the message left us in no doubt that this was not a request, so we all scarpered out of the front door posthaste. "Last one out is a poofter," yelled Scouse Crawford, as we fell over each other in an attempt to prove that we were not the effeminate one of the billet.

It was indeed Corporal Connolly who had issued the order as he stood on the roadway in front of the huts like a sentinel. "Hearcut toym," he said rather more loudly than was required. We would find out within a short period of time that he said everything rather more loudly than was required. "Yous teddy boys won't be yous teddy boys for much longer," he told us in his own inimitable fashion. He had a way of speaking that was all his own, though very Irish, quite unlike any accent I had ever heard before. I found it fascinating and could not wait for him to speak again. "The berber doesn't take requests," he told us. " 'e only knows 'ow to cut hear one wey," he went on. " T'morra yous will be issued wiv a berry, and the hear that shows below the edband belongs to me, anyfink above belongs to yous," he told us.

Jock McBride wanted to know what the hell the corporal was talking about as he could not understand a word the man said. At least, I think that is what Jock wanted to know, so I told him the corporal said that all the hair showing below the band of your beret was his and would be removed. Any above was your own and you could keep it. He looked at me with a puzzled expression on his face, so I just shrugged. When Jock and the corporal got talking together later on, the ensuing conversation had to be heard to be believed. It threw us all into hysterics.

We were lined up three abreast and marched, after a fashion, to the barber's hut. Short back and sides was given to, "Every mon Jack ov yous," as the corporal said. Each haircut took about thirty seconds, so the whole bunch of us was shorn in the time it takes to read the football results on a Saturday evening. It was like a factory production line turning out freshly minted boy airmen. The effect was devastating. The body coming out of the barber's hut was totally unrecognisable from the body going in. Scouse was before me, C's before H's remember, and I did not know him when he came out. His long, fair, curly hair had gone and it was as if a complete metamorphosis had taken place.

When my turn came I got cold feet and decided I would join the Red Cross or help old ladies to cross the road, anything that did not require such drastic action as this. "Arris, gerrin there," Corporal Connolly whispered not too gently in my ear. Half a minute later I looked just like the rest of the lads with my shaven head feeling and looking like one of the coconuts I had won at the fair on Golden Hill Park in a previous life. What happened to the hair above the 'edband'! Gone, disappeared without trace.

"Now yous are fit t' meet yous flight commander, seeing as yous are no longer teddy boys," Connolly told us. "But that will not be till t'morra mornin' after yous have all had yous breakfasiz," he went on. "Yous are all delicate blooms that need to be treated wiv care. I will treat yous wiv care, because from now on I am your muvver, your farver, your bruvver and your sister. If yous have any problems yous will bring them to me and I will sort them out just like yous muvvers used to do," he said.

Good God, I thought. I came all this way to get away from my mother and here she is in the guise of an Irish corporal! I do not really remember my mother sorting out many problems; causing them maybe, but sorting out, no; hopefully the corporal was better at it than she was.

We were then escorted to the bedding store and issued with four blankets, two sheets, two pillowslips and two pillows. I told the corporal I thought they had made a mistake with my issue. My bedding at home had been one sheet, two ex-army blankets, one with a large hole in it, and an old army greatcoat with most of the buttons missing. My pillow had been a bolster shared between our John and me that rarely had a cover on it. Being overwhelmed with the amount of bedding the issue clerk had given me convinced me he had made an error. The corporal thought I was being funny and said, "Arris, isn't it? I remember yous from before. Think yous are a comedian do we? Get fell in wiv the rest and let that be the last I 'ears from yous."

His grammar was wonderful and I promised myself I would try to learn to speak the way he did. Although it was hard to hide my embarrassment, maybe I managed it because the lads thought I was taking the Mickey out of authority and that went down well. "You've got some bottle," Scouse whispered to me, as we staggered back to the billet with our burden, thinking I had been joking about sheets and pillowslips. Seeing him out of the corner of my eye, he winked as if to say, "You'll do me pal."

Some time later, after making up our beds, Sergeant Lean appeared in the billet and screamed at us to be on our feet. He stood as straight as a post with his hands behind his back and made the following statement. "Right my lads, you are all delicate blooms that need to be treated with care. I will treat you with care, because from now on I am your mother, your father, your brother and your sister. If you have any problems you will bring them to me and I will sort them out just like your mother used to do."

I could not believe it. It was exactly the same speech Corporal Connolly had made to us earlier, but this time in the Queen's English. They really should have got their act together and decided who was going to say what, as I certainly did not need two mothers, fathers, brothers and sisters on top of those I had at home. The sergeant went on, "Tomorrow morning you will meet your flight commander,

Flight Lieutenant Morris. He is a gentleman of the first order, but will not stand for sloppiness, slovenliness or disorderly conduct. Play the game with him and he will play the game with you. He is a bomber pilot on ground duties for two years as a rest period from the pressures of flying, and I don't want any of you causing him stress he can well do without."

Great, I thought, that is all I need, a flight commander who has been grounded. This is likely to mean he will have a chip on his shoulder as big as Mont Blanc, as aircrew seldom like being taken off flying duties, especially to look after a bunch of brats.

No one slept very much that night, it being the first many of us had spent away from home. It was still dark when we were called from our beds by some lunatic blowing a bugle on the parade ground a little down the road from hut 77. Somebody said it was called reveille and it happened every morning at six o'clock.

After attending to our ablutions, we were lined up and marched off to get our 'breakfasiz' by Corporal Connolly. The mess was an oversized hut 77, painted with the same black paint. The food was good, but there again, any food was good as far as I was concerned. I was a growing boy needing sustenance and the RAF was fully aware of this. After our corn flakes, egg, bacon, fried bread, beans, toast and jam, washed down with a pint of tea drunk out of a pint size tin mug, we were introduced to our flight commander. He was a tall man, too tall for a pilot I thought. All the pilots I had previously met had been rather short, which helped them to fit more easily into the cockpit of an aircraft. He had a look of Gregory Peck and his movements were slow and deliberate. He said his name was Flight Lieutenant Morris and was so glad to meet us all. He continued in his best Oxbridge accent, "You are all delicate blooms................."

Did my ears deceive me! Alas no, it was the same speech, word for word, we had heard twice before. Whilst this may seem incredible, it is true and I can only assume they had all seen the same film and thought these words impressive. We all had a good laugh about this later whilst relaxing back in hut 77, but relaxation was not on the curriculum for RAF Boy Entrants.

***

EPILOGUE

For the next eighteen months, we were kept at it day and night. Bull nights, which meant cleaning the billet and making sure everything was spick and span, gleaming bright and dust free; marching; shooting on the rifle range; how to salute correctly; physical training; sports of all kinds but most importantly, how to keep the aircraft of the Royal Air Force flying. We were trained to be the ground crews of the future, those back room boys whose tasks are rarely seen but, nevertheless, are vital to the air defence of Britain and its protectorates.

However, no such silly patriotic thoughts ever entered my mind. All I wanted was a better life than I had previously known and it was to be found here with a bunch of lads who came from a diversity of backgrounds. They came from Scotland, Tyneside, Merseyside, Manchester, Somerset, Cornwall, London and all places south, as well as Northern Ireland and the Irish Republic. We blended together supremely well and settled into a new life as though it had been preordained. Things were good and the time of my life was had performing survival training in the Brecon Beacons in Wales and Bodmin Moor in Cornwall. I visited many RAF stations to see how they operated and flew in various aircraft to gain air experience which was great fun. A whole new world had opened up for me, a world far removed from the back entries of Upshaw and Gormless Gregory with his nicked biscuits.

It dawned on me that back then we had built a canoe, a raft, and our own version of formula one racing cars in the form of soapboxes, but had never attempted to build an aircraft. I wondered why? The silly, petty restrictions imposed here by those who had to be obeyed could be endured, having found a life full of adventure and comradeship where teamwork was a requisite part of everyday life and I loved every minute of it.

The following twelve years was spent in air force blue and during that time, I gradually lost touch with the gang I grew up with. I would find out later that Gormless Gregory went on to be a professional musician and still is as far as I am aware. I believe he still cannot read music! Skiver went into the mercantile marine as a radio officer but did not like the ocean; Don decided to be a teacher after a spell in the Royal Navy, where he was clumsy enough to fall off HMS Ark Royal whilst painting the ship's side. It was a more spectacular plunge than his fall from Kon Tiki but he got just as wet. However the outcome was more serious because he was charged with deserting his post without permission and placed on Captain's report; Dennis became a banker and misspent everyone's money and Jim emigrated to Canada, where I am told he died somewhere in the Rocky Mountains whilst studying the indigenous birds;

William Danson vanished completely and John O'Sullivan was last heard of in Singapore working as an engineer. I wonder if there are any orchards out there! His brother Rory is somewhere in Scotland, probably tending sheep. Of Len and Brian Jackson, I have no knowledge. Lynn and Anne both still live in the Upshaw area having married local lads who remained in situ. We still meet from time to time and swap memories. My siblings all married and had families of their own and I see little of them, apart from Lana who remains very dear to me and I see whenever I can. Many of the other characters mentioned have long since died but their being lives on in my memory.

Sally, Duke and Arnold, those Alsatian dogs who seemed to be ever present in my childhood, have long gone to the great kennel in the blue beyond, and as far as Arnold is concerned, I could not think of a better place for him to be.

So, I did eventually manage to drain that swamp but the alligators left a few scars to remind me of where I came from. Oscar Wilde's stars were not so far away after all and the feeling of wanting something better was eventually sated. You see, dreams sometimes do come true if you try hard enough. The road is not always easy but can be well worth it if you make the effort.

And what happened to the upholsterer's daughter? Well --that's another story.

***

Freddie Harris served for twelve years in the Royal Air Force, 'holidaying' in locations as diverse as Cyprus, Libya and North Wales. On demobilisation, he joined H.M. Prison Service where he worked for twenty-three years in Strangeways Prison in Manchester, until a heart condition forced his retirement. He then moved to the Lake District, the ancestral home of his maternal grandparents. He writes as a hobby and talks to visitors at Brantwood House, the last home of John Ruskin, that great Victorian. Freddie has written a lecture on Ruskin and presents it to whoever is bold enough to listen!